Hatter's Shop

Krista Coleman

Hatter's Shop

Krista Coleman

ISBN-13: 9798373453875

Contents

Of Fidelity and Fascination 1

Of Fire and Madness...17

Of Weddings and Wonder..31

Of Quests and Companions 48

Of Bonds and Blunders..62

Of Dungeons and Desires..81

Of War and Love...100

Chapter One:
Of Fidelity and Fascination

I t was one month before her older sister's wedding and all Alice could think of was finding a groom better suited for Margaret. Meanwhile, all her sister and mother could think of were the little details that would give her new family a firm upstanding place in society.

"Isn't the continuation of our father's legacy firm and upstanding enough?" Alice mused aloud. Her voice was readily caught by the ear of her kin.

"Alice, dear," her mother shook her head, "that would be *our* family. Your sister Margaret is going to establish a new one. She'll have a new surname."

Alice looked to her sister, "What's wrong with the one you've already got?"

"Alice," her sister laughed. She was soft, matronly, and beautiful. Alice was certain that she could obtain any man she wanted; anyone would be better than her than her cheating fiancé, Luke. "Society has established the practice of taking your husband's name as expected and proper. Someday soon you'll have a new name, too."

"I will not!" Alice spoke indignantly as they wove around the people on the busy London streets. She was trying to keep up with the excited pace of her family. "I like my name just the way it is, thank you."

When Alice's mother and sister stopped abruptly, she had to steer herself from plowing into them. "Ah, here we are!" said her mother, ignoring Alice's statement. "Hatter's Shop. All the ladies will be needing fascinators for the event."

Through the wide front windows, Alice stared at the curios with wonderment. There were hats made of soft felt, light yarns, lacey bonnets, and large-brimmed statements of hats. The small circlets with feathers and beads caught her eye and stirred her fancy.

"Come along, Alice." Her mother grabbed her by the wrist and pulled her inside. "You'll be the model for the bridesmaids. Now, I've heard that the man is a little eccentric," her nose shriveled, "but you will hold your tongue, won't you? ...Alice?" Her voice wavered as she noticed her child's hand was no longer in her own. *What would she do with that curious girl?* Or, rather, she was now a curious woman. She kept forgetting that her hard-to- tie-down daughter had recently turned twenty four.

Alice walked around the shop to get a better feel for the creations. She wondered if she would even be wearing a fascinator at all, once she found the strength to tell her sister of Luke's observed infidelity. Her fingers trailed along the samples that adorned mannequin heads in a melancholy way; from scratchy wool to feathery softness. The bobbles rolled pleasantly beneath her fingertips.

She paused in her tracks; there was a material she'd never seen before. It was a curled, burnished orange type of frayed yarn. It was strangely beautiful and impossibly tangled. She tentatively stroked the ends and twirled them between her fingers.

"That tickles, you know." Green eyes, with flecks of warm brown and gold, looked up at her from behind the shelf.

"Oh!" Alice realized her hands were still woven into the man's hair. She swiftly retracted them to her sides. "What were you doing there? I thought you were a bust model, like the others." His skin was so pale that she wasn't entirely sure he wasn't a mannequin.

He stood, tall and silent, with an impossibly wistful look on his face. *How strange.*

"Oh, there you are, Alice!" said Margaret, "I see you've found Mister Hatter. He'll be assisting us with the fascinators."

The hatter did not answer her sister, nor did he glance in her direction. He kept his eyes trained on Alice as he moved towards her, and around her in an appraising circle. In all her years, Alice had not received the romantic gaze of her peers. The constant comparison to a prized woman like Margaret had prevented that. Alice had never known a gaze to reach out and touch her, and yet this one had engulfed her. She panicked and gave her mother a beseeching look.

"Oh, come now, Alice. Genius is... well, it's a different breed." Her eyebrows crumpled in assessment. "Margaret and I will be heading out to run some other errands for the wedding. We know that we are leaving you in highly capable hands."

Margaret gave her sister a curious smile. "Don't worry, we'll be back before supper."

"But Margaret! Mother!" Alice took a step after them.

"Be a good girl, Alice! It's for your sister." The door chimed shut behind them.

For Margaret. Alice's stomach dropped. She'd heard those words before. The memory of Luke flirting with the maid came back to her with a sinking feeling: *Please, for Margaret. Don't tell her. She loves me. She wants to marry me. You don't want her to be unhappy, do you?* Conflict bubbled in her stomach. No one deserved an eternity with a disloyal dog; least of all her sister.

Alice took a seat in the chair in front of the mirror. Her stomach lifted, along with a lock of her hair, as the hatter tenderly pulled a length of it between his fingertips. Reflected in the looking-glass, she noted the thimble on his thumb and a pin cushion at his wrist. A measuring tape hung around his neck. It was the twentieth century, but the hatter's style leaned towards the eighteenth. His jacket, trousers, and a waistcoat were made of a strange fabric woven to be almost iridescent. An ascot was pinned with a peacock feather at his neck. The hatter certainly was a different breed; something she had never seen before.

Alice shivered as the strands of hair were brushed from the back of her neck. She felt strangely bare as the hatter stood there looking at her nape. His head tilted, as if he were imagining her measurements and committing them to memory.

"Teatime!" His shout broke the silence and rattled her nerves.

Alice's thick blonde curls fell heavily against her back. She turned to watch the hatter, in awe, as he took a seat at a work table draped in fabrics. He poured one pipping cup from a kettle settled under some samples. He knocked babbles down in a flurry as he grabbed a plate hidden by a large top hat. The hatter blew on the steam rising from his mug, staring at Alice all the while.

"What?" Alice's eyebrows knit together. "Do you... want me to sit down?"

"Won't you join me? It *is* teatime, after all." He looked at her as if she were the odd one.

4

"Oh. Of course." It was better to go along with his game than against it. Margaret really wanted this prestigious man as her hatter. Alice got up and sat to his left.

"No, no! That seat is much too uncomfortable. Here, try the one to my right."

She nodded stiffly and took the suggested seat.

He was about to take another sip when he put his cup down. "Silly me," he laughed, "this cup is more of an Alice, isn't it? I have a Hatter mug in the cupboard." His chair moved on the floor with a squeak. She was about to decline when he pushed the cup in front of her. A small splash hit the table. "Ah-ha!" he shouted after retrieving the item. Then, he took a new seat to her right.

Alice couldn't help but laugh at the absurdity of it all.

"There we are," he said with a soft grin.

"What?" She picked up her dainty porcelain cup.

"That's the first time your smile has shown its face all day."

"You mean that my face has smiled?"

"No, my Alice. A smile has a face all of its own." He beamed then.

She had to agree.

After a brief teatime, it was back to business. Alice must have been sitting for hours as the hatter's fingers deliberately mapped her scalp. The light friction of his hands against her skin was driving her nearer and nearer to insanity. The madness felt like a tickling sensation in her chest.

"I don't understand why you don't make use of the measuring tape around your neck."

"Numbers are fickle things," he hummed. "I prefer to feel."

"If you aren't measuring, then, just what are you doing to my head?" Alice jerked forward at his laughter. She looked back at the slender, broad-shouldered man in accusation. "You've gone mad, haven't you?"

He laughed louder, as if it were the funniest thing in the world.

She didn't catch the joke. "What are you laughing at?"

"Your angry Alice face." He wiped a happy tear from his eye. "It would seem that *your* madness is more apparent than mine."

"I take it back;" she huffed, "you're an absolute loon."

"Of course not," he said staunchly. "I'm quite partial to a raven."

"Are you going to make me a hat or not?"

"Not." His full brows furrowed.

Her mouth opened and closed in fear. She turned to him. "What? Why?"

Hatter's warm palms traveled over her shoulders. She could feel that tickling sensation inside her once more. "It's not a hat, Alice," he shook his head softly. "It's a fascinator: a fascinating fascinator!"

"You're right," she laughed against her indignation. "Now I've gone mad. I hope it isn't catching."

"Oh, I should hope so." His eyes traveled over her face. "Crimson looks *awfully* good on you."

Alice's heart leapt to her throat when she heard her mother's voice at the door. "Alice, dear, we're back." She had several bags in tow. "How was your appointment? Is everything going to be on schedule?"

The hatter took a breath, readying to speak.

Alice looked at him fretfully. She couldn't trust him not to make her family nervous. After all, he hadn't properly measured her head. He hadn't drawn up any designs all day. Alice grasped his wrist to stop him from speaking. "Hatter and I are going to meet again, tomorrow." His gaze lingered at the fingers on his skin. "Tomorrow?" He raised a thick brow.

"Tomorrow; we'll have tea," she nodded.

"Oh! I do love tea," he cheered.

"I figured as much," Alice said, mainly to herself.

"That's an excellent idea, Alice," her sister smiled. "Now, come along for supper."

As Alice's fingers unraveled, she couldn't shake the guilty feeling that had formed in her.

The next day, Alice appeared in front of a dark storefront. "Of *course*." She pinched the skin between her eyebrows in frustration. The day was Sunday: most shops would be closed. "I was a fool for saying that we would meet up. I don't even know why I showed up. He probably knew it was a stupid excuse to stall for time since we made no progress on the fascinators." Upon hearing footsteps, she looked up.

"What are we looking for?" the hatter chimed from behind her; his frame was reflected in the glass of the closed shop. He cupped his hands and peered inside, inadvertently pressing her up against the storefront.

"Hatter!" Alice stood a head or so below him. Her back could feel his body heat through the fabric before she turned, "Hatter, I was looking for you!"

"Oh no! You've found me too soon," he looked distraught. "Should I hide again?"

"No, Hatter," she laughed. "But, I *am* afraid I've come at the wrong time."

"Is it tomorrow?"

"...Yes."

"High Tea?"

"I should say so. But it's not like you want to open your shop just for some tea."

"That would be absurd. I'd rather not have tea time in a shop if I can help it: too constricting."

"Then," she looked down while still encased in his arms, "I'll be going."

He nodded, "I'll go, too." He hooked an arm around her own and strolled determinedly down the street.

"Hatter- I meant that I was going to get out of your hair! I know my presence here must be bothersome."

"I don't mind when you play with my hair. You're not bothersome, Alice. All the opposite words: Calming. Pleasing. Pleasant. Delightful."

"I see," she flushed. Then she looked up at him. "Where are we going?"

"Why, isn't it obvious?" He chuckled, "For tea."

The two found themselves in front of an odd building in the woods. It was as if the math were all wrong, but the angles found a way to work themselves out. It was a black and white Tudor style building with a steep and slanted roof, an elaborate brick chimney, half-timbering, white stucco, and an embellished wooden door. Colorful flowers fell from vines, like streamers from each window box. *Was it some sort of quaint tea shop she'd never seen before? The foundation was odd, but it was welcoming enough.*

"After you." Hatter held the tilted door ajar.

Alice felt wary, but her curiosity pushed her forward. She'd always know it was her biggest flaw. Once indoors, she noted a rectangular kitchen table dressed in too many place settings. There was a reading nook with several books opened part way, as if the reader were combining all stories in one sitting. A cozy fireplace from which the kettle was already keening. Two mismatched tweed and tartan couches bordered a thickly woven rug.

She soon realized she was not in a tea shop. "Hatter," Alice stepped back towards the threshold, "are we in your home?"

"Not my **home**, per say," Hatter retrieved the kettle from the fire, "but it is my house."

He always seemed to speak in riddles. It was a good thing she had a quick wit. "*Your* house?"

"I should say so," Hatter grinned as he poured the tea. "One lump or four?"

"Hatter, I didn't know that we were coming to your house." Alice stalled.

"No?" his brows rose in confusion.

"I thought we'd be meeting in a shop. Some would say it's indecent for an unwed woman and man to be alone at home together."

"I see..." his face fell. "I apologize if I've done something to offend you."

"No, not at all!" Alice steadied herself. "The notion *is* antiquated. Though, I would have liked to know where we were headed. I don't mind being alone with you. I mean, we are somewhat acquaintances. I would even say that we're becoming friends. Aren't we?"

"I should say so," Hatter placed the tray on the wooden table next to the couches. He looked up curiously. "Does that mean we should be wed?"

"No!" Alice responded in a voice too shrill for her liking. "It's all right for two unwed people to be alone together. It's not a crime." After she calmed, she glanced at him. "You really *are* a mad hatter, aren't you?"

Hatter spilled some tea. "Does that mean you remember?"

"Remember what?" her brows wrinkled, "that you're mad?"

Hatter breathed out through his nose as he returned to the tray of tea. "We should drink it before it gets cold." He touched the cup.

"Thank you," she looked up at him, concerned. "You've got a terrible look on your face. Was it something I said? I promise not to call you mad anymore, if that's the case."

"It's not that, Alice. Afterall, I *am* mad. All the best people are. I just don't want you to be feeling indecent. Perhaps I should return to my home."

"Hatter," she examined his pained expression, "you're not making any sense with all this talk about houses and homes. Aren't we sitting in your home at this moment?"

"No, Alice," he implored her to see his reason. "This world is *your* home."

"World?" A chill crept down her spine. "I know that you and I are different. But are we so different that we inhabit different worlds?"

"I- well- quite frankly, yes."

"More so than men are from Mars and women from Venus?"

He snorted a laugh. "I wish it were that simple."

"Tell me, then. If not here, where is your home?"

His eyes sought hers. "It doesn't work if I tell you." He slumped into his tartan chair. "If I take you there, you'll never see it. And you'll never remember. You'll have to find your own way, Alice." He glanced up at her. "I'd only meant to guide you to the door." He turned his face from hers in shame. "But, then, you reached out and touched me-"

"Hatter..." She couldn't stand to see him so forlorn. Even if he was nearly a stranger, it broke her heart. "I'm sorry. I don't know what to say."

"Say that you'll remember," the hatter spoke, silently.

"I can try." She brought her hand to his in an effort to comfort him. "Come now, let's take our tea out in the garden and get some fresh air. Shall we?"

He chewed on his lip. She knew he had wanted to say something, but decided against it with a nod.

Not for the first time, Alice wondered if the hatter truly was mad. He'd divulged to her that he thought he was from another world. Maybe he did it to entice her. Whether or not he believed it himself was another story. Yet, Alice felt the spark, an echo of truth, every time Hatter inadvertently brushed her skin. *If he was such a stranger, then why did she feel this indescribable pull? Why did it feel like he held onto a part of her that she had been missing?*

She waited for the moments when their eyes caught one another in his shop. Looking past the outdated clothing and unkempt hair, the hatter was a handsome man. He was tall and lean muscled, with jewel-like eyes and a pleasing facial structure that was both soft and strong. Her eyes lingered on his lips, and she thought, *maybe she could...* Alice shook her head free of the daydream. *His madness was catching.*

Alice hadn't known she was susceptible to persuasion. Yet, the more time she spent with Hatter, the more she was beginning to believe in his delusion. Logic stated that there was no way another world existed within her own. Such a thing was physically impossible. It was scaring her that she could believe that; that **he** could believe it. If she wanted to keep her sanity, she needed to never see the man again. Margaret could find fascinators at another hat shop. Even if her sister hated her; even if it cost her the dear friendship that was developing, it would be worth it not to lose herself.

"Alice?" A knock came at her door. "Alice!" The knock came harder.

"Mother?" she mumbled against her pillow.

"Alice Everly," her mother entered in a tizzy, "you are late for your appointment with the hatter. We can't lose this man's business! And, if you don't mind me saying," her mother said smugly, "I don't think you would much like him losing interest in you."

"Mother!" Alice forgot her tiredness and sat up. "Absolutely not! He's a loon. Or- well- a raven. I've decided not to see that man again."

"Alice, dear," her mother cooed as she sat on the bed, "he runs a prosperous business. Would it be so bad if you got together?"

"It would!" Alice huffed. Though she did not know why she felt so adamantly against it. She felt guilty for the images that coupling with the hatter brought to mind. "He's absolutely mad: *a mad hatter!*"

"I see," her mother nodded. "But he's treated you so delicately. Many boys have balked at your strength, or treated you roughly- like one of their own. He cherishes you. The way he looks at you, it's almost as if he's known you for a very long time."

Alice bit her lip. "Well, he hasn't. We shan't speak on this anymore."

"All right, darling," Her mother agreed. "Then I hope you won't mind that Clarence has asked you to your sister's rehearsal dinner. We've been neighbors and business associates with the Aldens for a while now. It would do well to reinforce the connection."

"I..." Alice stared at her mother, unsure of how to rebuke. She didn't know why it felt so wrong. The very thought of dinner with her neighbor seemed to border on infidelity. Yet, she had no one to be faithful to. Maybe she was unfairly comparing herself to her sister's fiancé. Though she and the hatter had been on several outings, she wasn't being courted. They were just friends. "I see."

"Well, my dear, you will let me know by this evening, won't you?" her mother implored.

"Of course."

"Good," her mother patted her arm. "Now, get up and get dressed."

Alice did not know how she had managed to get dragged to Hatter's Shop once more. She couldn't even recall the taste of breakfast. Yet, there she was, in the vicinity of the man she had sworn never to see again. Her family must have wanted her to become certifiably insane. She didn't know how much longer she could stay grounded in the sway of Hatter's heady presence.

The man in question surveyed swatches of fabric as he chewed at a pin in his mouth. "Ah, here it is!" he pointed, "I would know it anywhere: **the** blue." Hatter grasped the handling sheers at his work table.

"You speak of the color as if it were a friend."

"Well, we *are* well acquainted," Hatter smiled.

"Acquainted? You mean, like how you and I are friends?" Alice admired the tender work of his hands. He'd become prestigious over a short span of time for a reason.

Hatter looked at her with surprise. Then his expression became befuddled. "Alice, has something happened to your muchness?"

"My- my what?" her throat was dry.

"Your muchness looks different today." He placed the pin from his mouth into the waiting fabric, which he then abandoned on the table. "Yes, I should say so. You've misplaced it."

"What are you talking about?" she yawned after a long night spent thinking about her impending insanity.

"It's escaping you as we speak!" He swiftly placed two fingers over her lips.

She suddenly felt more awake. The jolting sensation from her stomach was reflected in her eyes.

"Oh! There it is." Hatter withdrew his hand with a grin.

"...Muchness?" Alice brought her fingers to her lips as the hatter returned to his work.

"Yes, Alice. You have the most muchness out of anybody there is."

"I see," she breathed. "Is that good?"

"The best." From behind him, she could see the blush creep over his ears. He soon returned to work with the pale blue fascinator on her head.

She wondered if they had such things in the hatter's imaginary world. Or, if people even got married there. Curiosity got the best of her once more. "Hatter," Alice explored, "do people get married where you're from?" She could feel his hands stall in her hair.

"Not really, Alice. Why do you ask?"

14

"Well, if someone should be in love with another member of, erm," she struggled to come up with the word, "*your realm*, then what would happen?"

"They would tell the queen."

"You have a queen?" Alice blinked. Maybe he was from England, after all.

"One White Queen and one bloody braggart of a Red Queen: the Queen of Hearts." He paused to calm down. "Oh! There's also a Duchess. She has a pleasant countenance; at least when she's not around pepper. It makes people hot-tempered, you know."

"I see."

"If two people should profess their love to one another," the hatter continued, "then the chosen queen would hold a ceremony to bind them."

"I didn't know you were from a kingdom. Are there knights?"

"Indeed. And days."

"Hatter!" Alice tittered. "You know what I mean."

His emerald eyes peered down over her head. "I'm sorry. What were we talking about, again?"

His peering over her was reminiscent of someone else for a moment: someone with a wide smile and curious eyes. The image faded quickly. She shook her head to clear her mind. "Anyway, in this society, before the day of the wedding is a rehearsal dinner. It's a night where everyone toasts to the couple. Then, they practice what will happen at the wedding in the following days. Guests often attend with a date."

"A date? I suppose it's better than a fig."

"No, not the fruit. A *date*, as in going out with a person of romantic interest."

"I see." He stepped away to observe the progress of her fascinator.

"Clarence has asked me to be his date to Margaret's wedding rehearsal dinner."

Hatter's face darkened a moment before he turned to his workstation. "...I see."

Alice's face grew hot. "I mean, I've never liked him. I'd rather not go with him."

Hatter turned back to her with wide eyes. "If not him, then who would be your fig?"

"Again, it's called a date, Hatter. And I was hoping- well, I was hoping it would be you." There it was: the whisper of her oncoming insanity. This was not at all what she had expected to happen with her day. The sane part of her brain was calling her every name in the book. She shouldn't have mentioned Clarence. She should have faced the situation and attended with him to please her mother. But the look on the hatter's face at her spur-of-the-moment decision was worthwhile.

"Me?" He pressed a finger to his chest as his brows rose.

All Alice could do was nod. Would he think of her as brash for asking him out?

"Oh, Alice!" He picked her up, locking his arms at the back of her skirt and spinning her around. "You've made me so happy!"

She stopped her breathing and all she could do was gape. *How was he so strong for such a slim man?* "You can put me down now, Hatter."

"Yes," he nodded slowly in recognition of his actions, "of course." He placed her down gently. "Forgive me, I got excited," he said shyly. "No one's ever asked me on a- on a *date* before."

She smiled at his correct use of the term. "If you behave, perhaps I'll ask you on a fig," she teased. At his puzzled expression, all she could do was laugh.

Chapter Two:
Of Fire and Madness

I t was another rainy day on the streets of London. Droplets traveled down the storefront of Hatter's Shop, pooling at the molding, and finding their way to the river in the gutter. Again, Alice felt his broad hands lift the hair from her neck and a shiver traveled up her spine. Warmth blossomed within her. *How was it possible to feel such a way so quickly?* She smiled to herself. If she were being honest, she'd felt it the moment she'd run her fingers through his wild orange hair.

She closed her eyes as she listened to him work, hearing the thread spooling from somewhere within his sleeve, listening to his teeth cut the cord, his steady breath as he passed it through the eye of a needle. A hum of appreciation came as his cold fingers trailed from the front of her to the back, appropriately adjusting the garment in a business-like fashion. When he brushed her neck, she took in a sharp breath and shivered once more.

"This store *is* a bit drafty. Are you all right, Alice?"

"I'm quite all right," she blushed. "You're doing a great job. Don't stop, please."

He heard something in her voice that made him shiver as well. *Oh Alice, tell me to continue forever and I'll do so.* Hatter let Alice's hair fall freely on her back once more. She had such soft smooth skin: a contrast to his callouses. Her skin was warm where he was cold. She was the perfect Alice-size, just fitting beneath his chin when she stood. Her hands would fit within his hands, her waist would be level to his own. His Alice, **the** Alice, seemed to compliment him so nicely. Not that he would ever inform her.

"Hatter," Alice stalled, "I have to tell you something."

"Anything." He abandoned his thoughts and straightened at her sudden seriousness.

"I have a secret that's been eating me alive, and I need your advice."

"I shall feed myself to the secret, if you desire it."

"That won't be necessary," she smiled sadly. "Hatter, you've made such a lovely fascinator but- unfortunately- I don't think that there should be a wedding."

"Why not?" he questioned.

"I saw my sister's fiancé flirting with another woman. I haven't told her yet."

"You haven't?" his brows furrowed.

"No. I want her to be happy. He said that he wants her to be happy, and she's happiest with him."

"That sounds like a paradox. How can she be happy if her happiness is not true?"

Alice frowned and played with her skirt. "I wasn't sure that you'd understand."

"I suppose not. What would you want if you were in her situation?"

"If I were her, I would have liked to know. At least I could make my own decision from there."

"Then, it's settled. Allow her that opportunity."

Alice looked down at her hands. "Even if it ruins her future? Even if she hates me?"

"Your sister loves you dearly. She could never truly hate you, even if she says she does. She might be cross for a while, but it's not really you that she's cross at. Is it? You could never ruin a future that wasn't meant to be."

"I suppose you're right. I feel a bit clearer on what I should do. I'm glad I could talk to you about it, Hatter."

"You can talk all you like, Alice. I'm glad I have you to listen to."

Alice smiled, comforted.

"And if Margaret decides to have a wedding," Hatter gave one final tap at the garment on Alice's head, "then she will have some lovely fascinators to look at." He stood back, near the mirror, to admire his work.

"How-" she gulped in anticipation, "How does it look?"

"Alone, it's nothing. On you, it's simply ravishing." He clasped his hands in approval with a smile at his lips.

In the looking glass, she noted the embarrassed flush on her face. Her eyes took to admiring the powdery blue of her off-oval fascinator. The tiny mock veil resembled a spider web. It was covered in a dew of glass beads and crystals. "It's brilliant!" she glowed. At least Margaret would have something to enjoy.

He grinned at her words of praise. "I'm so happy that you approve."

"Will all the ladies have one like this?" She touched the fabric delicately.

"No, Alice," he shook his head. "Yours is the only one."

"But, what about the bridesmaids?" Alice stuttered in a panic. "I'll have to hand them out: the rehearsal dinner is tomorrow! "

He gave a small laugh, "They each have their own. I've provided them already."

"Oh," Alice paused at the added information. "I thought I would be the model for them. Did they each meet with you?"

"They did." He cleaned his station. "They visited my shop after your appointments."

"Those were some late nights." Alice didn't know why her heart was trying to jump up her throat. "You had to have gotten to know some of them pretty well." Margaret had many friends that were just as warm and matronly as she was. "Did you meet anyone special?"

"I did," he smiled. "I made some new friends. One lady even asked me over for tea, but then I remembered what you said about unwed men and women being alone in a house together."

Alice wished she never had an imagination. A flighty sensation grew in her stomach. Other girls had experienced the feel of his fingertips. Other girls had spent time admiring the oddly handsome man. *Other girls had asked him out.* And he would have said *yes* if she hadn't thrown a wrench into the works. Was she as special in his eyes as her mind had made her out to be?

"Alice?" Hatter looked confused.

She carefully removed the fascinator from her head and set it aside on the worktable. She knew exactly what this feeling was: jealousy. She was only surprised that it happened so soon. She didn't know why her feelings for the man had grown so strong over a short amount of time. She didn't have a right to capitalize on a busy business owner's time. She didn't have a right to capitalize on a *handsome single man's* time.

Logically, she knew he was only doing his job. Alice didn't **want** to feel this way. She needed to get some fresh air to become a rational human being again. "I have to step out for a moment." Alice turned towards the door as thoughts flooded her head. *Did you tell them about your realm as well? Did you win them over, too? Were all men the same? Would her situation be just the same as Margaret's some day?*

"Alice?" Hatter's voice was as small as a dormouse.

The rain began to pick up; a gentle breeze brought the mist to her face. *Why do you care so much? You said it yourself, he's mad. Alice- is he making you mad, too?*

"Alice!" Hatter was out of breath behind her.

She realized that she had made it to the tree line without thinking.

He approached her, gently wiping a trailing droplet from her cheek.

"It's the rain. I'm fine." She breathed. "I just need a moment."

"Are you sure? Did you eat or drink anything strange today? The last time you did, your tears were enough to fill the sea."

"What are you talking about?" She turned, aggravated at her lack of understanding; at his unrelenting presence witnessing her falling apart. "*I never know what it is you're talking about!*"

He looked hurt for a moment. Then his back straightened. "That *is exactly* how I feel."

The weight of the water pulled at their hair and clothing. Rain dotted their faces as they searched one another's gaze.

Alice spoke, "I wish I understood you. Or, that I could help you to understand. But I can't; I can't even understand my *stupid* self."

"I won't have you speaking ill about my Alice," his brow furrowed.

"*Am* I your Alice? There are so many girls named Alice in this world. What if she's out there and you're wasting your time on me? And if she is, what is the reason for you to swindle me, or those other Alices, into believing you come from another world?" She paused. "You know what? Why should it matter? *I don't even know you!*"

He gave a sad smile before his arms wrapped tentatively around her shoulders. She was lost in the heat of his skin through wet linen. "*You know me*, my Alice. You know me better than anyone else. That's why I had to find you again."

"That doesn't make any sense!" she spoke against the lump in her throat.

"Yes, it does, Alice. You've only forgotten. I'm in there somewhere."

"That's impossible."

"You're awfully good at impossibilities."

"How long have I *known* you?" Her eyes raked him with suspicion.

"Well, we met when I was a smaller Hatter, and you were a smaller Alice."

"Not in England."

"No." He shook his head. "Not in England."

"How could that be? I've never left its shores."

"My world is within its shores. It's just not on the same plane as yours."

"I'm so confused," Alice's mind reeled. She needed to think. "Hatter?"

"Hm?"

"I need to sit down." The gray skies rumbled above them. "And we need to get out of this storm. Can we sit by your fire to warm up?"

"But," he panicked, "you said that it would be indecent. I know how uncomfortable it would make you to-"

"It's all right, Hatter," she stopped him from explaining. "I don't mind." And truthfully, she didn't.

Alice sat on the strange, yet comfortable, tweed sofa near the fire. She was a bit chilly in her bra, skirt slip, and pantyhose. She and the hatter had placed their outerwear near the flames while the storm continued to rage outside. Her body was covered in gooseflesh, so she held her hot tea closer on her lap. What was once a drizzle had become a deluge outside. Thunder rumbled somewhere over the distant meadows.

As she sipped her orange pekoe, Alice's eyes came to rest on the clinging of the hatter's shirt tucked into his high-waisted trousers. With his buttoned waistcoat and wool jacket discarded, she could see the outline of his taut frame through the wet fabric. Alice looked away, guiltily, as she felt a heat at her core that was much warmer than her tea. As she placed the cup back in its saucer on the table, she wondered what she was meant to do with her hands. She settled on folding them in her lap.

Hatter purposefully stared into the flames by the stone fireplace. Leaving a cup of fresh tea untouched on the table was unlike him. He was making her curiouser and curiouser. "Hatter?" Alice called.

"Alice?" His face met hers in profile. His eyes seemed almost golden in the firelight.

"Is something the matter? You've left your tea untouched." She tilted her head to try and catch his gaze, but he returned it to the fire. She frowned. "Why won't you look at me?"

"I would like to respect your modesty."

She looked down at herself for a moment. Another woman had asked him out, but had he ever gone further than that? His innocence made her believe otherwise. She had been with a few men, exploring each other's bodies. But she never liked one enough to stay for long. Just how experienced was her hatter in the ways of love? Could his propriety be an act? She wanted to find out. "Is it me, or does it," she spoke in a whisper, "feel as if this tea won't quench your thirst?"

Hatter's neon eyes turned back to her in that instant, wide and uncertain. He blinked a few times before looking down once more. He paused for a moment. "Yes."

Her heart pumped and swelled. She could feel the thickness of her pulse as she stood. Alice could see the bob of Hatter's throat as he turned to face her.

"Alice?" his voice was meek as he searched her face.

She was almost afraid to meet his honest eyes with her erotic intentions. "What should we do about that?"

He let out a quick and funny laugh in that moment, before turning back to the fire. "I haven't the slightest idea."

"You don't?" Maybe a kiss would quiet her curiosity, the absurd pangs of jealousy in her stomach. Maybe the feeling of her lips could place her above the other girls he called friends. Maybe a kiss could bring her some sanity... *Maybe*. She wanted so much more than a kiss. Could she stop at that? Would he want her to? She wanted to claim him and keep him all to herself. She wanted to find out what type of body was under those clothes. The wanting was killing her. She couldn't let this opportunity pass her by. She couldn't let another woman snatch him from under her nose. Alice set her resolve and began to walk towards him, "Because it sounds as if you do."

He twitched at the warmth of her hand on his damp shoulder. "Alice," he spoke almost warningly, "I know very well how *I* feel. But, it may be different from you."

She attempted to catch his shifting gaze once more. "What's the harm in a kiss?"

"My Alice," his face drained as it faced the fire, "you haven't the slightest idea."

"Hatter?" Patience was never Alice's virtue. "Please. I want you to look at me."

She was unprepared for the hunger in his searing gaze. "I fear that is what I want as well..."

His desperate eyes sought hers for understanding as she stepped forward to capture his mouth in hers. A light moan escaped him at the contact; one she nearly echoed. It was so pretty that she needed to hear it again. She pressed herself deeper into the kiss as her tongue traveled over his, tasting the warmth of the tea he'd left behind.

His heart sang. *She'd kissed him! Oh, Alice, could this mean? Could you?* No, he told himself, don't get too excited- it was likely a custom he'd seen in her world. *Were there kisses among friends?* It was so hard to understand her society. He was only certain that he loved her, and he loved her muchly.

Hatter's hands traveled across the bare skin of Alice's arms, up the curve of her shoulders to her neck and further to cup her chin and nape. He could never keep his fingers far from her scalp. He knew if he pulled her into him, if he exerted the sheer desire he felt, that she would fly away. His Alice was a flighty bird: a most beautiful, exciting, exquisite bird. She was one he could never hope or dream to contain in a cage. While he was elated, he was absolutely, unequivocally afraid. His heart beat against his ribcage as he tasted her. His fears were answered as she pulled away.

"Do you like me?" her kissed lips questioned.

He swooned at the notion that he was the one that made them look that way. "Most certainly."

She smiled: a bright smile with all her muchness. It was the way that an Alice should smile. And he knew, with seeping dread, that it was must past the word *like*. He would do anything- any impossibility- just to make her smile that way again.

Alice removed her warm hand from his shoulder. "May I?" she asked as she found the bottom of his shirt.

"Yes, please," his voice came out husky.

She carefully took the shirt tails out of his pants and allowed the cold fabric to slide across his skin. It perked his pecs as she tossed it on to a rack by the fire. His frame was like a marble statue. "We should let that dry."

His eyes roved over her face with curiosity. He could never predict what she would do next.

She kissed his clavicle as he let out a breathy noise that made her heart race. "I've never been with anyone like you."

"Is that a good thing?" he glanced down at his hands, still tangled in her hair at the base of her neck.

"You're impossibly perfect," she trailed her hands over his hairless chest and down the dimpled ridges of his midsection.

Hatter leaned into her touch, as if it sustained him. "If I am, then you're marveliferous, Alice."

"Marveliferous?" she asked. "Is that even a word?"

"Indeed. It means *beyond perfection*."

Her dark honeyed eyes sparkled as she looked up at him. "You really think so?"

"I know so," he hummed. "I've known that for a long time."

She lightly kissed his lips, tugging his flesh between her teeth before she parted. "Thank you." She leaned in to kiss him again.

The backs of his fingers ghosted over her exposed flesh, causing her bra strap to fall from her shoulder. "Is this all right?" he asked.

"It feels good," she arched into him, prompting his hand to her breast as the fire sparked and birchwood crackled beside them.

He took a sharp breath at the sensation of her pebbled nipple as his fingers searched under the cup of her bra. He felt himself growing madder by the minute. He wasn't sure if he was lost in a dream. He didn't want to wake up, if he was. His cool lips kissed her warm throat, drinking her, "Alice, my Alice..."

She sighed and melted into him. The way he toyed with her had her body humming and core throbbing. She wanted him, even more than she thought she did. The insanity was evident in the aching of her body. *Maybe there was harm in a kiss.* She was losing herself to his madness if her jealousy drove her this far. But, maybe there was more to this series of events; this persistent wanting feeling.

What did she really want from this man- this hatter? She only knew that she didn't want to hurt him or herself. Sex complicated friendships, and he had grown to be someone she could rely on; to confide in. Fear of losing him leapt in her throat. She pulled back to see the desperation in his eyes, and it scared her how much she could need him as well. She needed to stop and take stock of her situation. "Look," she turned to the window, "the rain has stopped."

"So it has." Hatter didn't know whether to laugh or cry. He had tasted her muchness, basked in it even, and now he would have to let her go. It was like letting go of a very good treacle tart. Even if he was only an experiment, a conquest, or a curiosity- he would let her use him. He would let her use him to her very best: until all of his muchness belonged to her.

"Oh! My blouse is dry!" She touched the fabric on the rack. "Maybe we should get dressed now?" she said, as if her mouth hadn't been on his own only a moment before. The hatter examined his coat on the rack by the fire. It was still damp. *Alice*, his heart sank, *have we gone too fast? We must have, if you are in such a hurry to be off.* A worrisome thought crossed his mind: *perhaps she didn't like the taste of him half as much as he did of her.*

In her struggle to pull on her skirt over her slip, she stumbled into the hatter's bare torso. Her hands caught his biceps. His hands caught her under the elbows. He gave a soft laugh of understanding. *How was it that she found herself in this predicament, again? How did she become so attached to an oddly charming man?* He made her heart beat, her knees buckle, and he made her believe in impossibilities: he made her a fool.

"Careful, Alice," he helped her regain her balance. "There's a fire."

Careful, indeed. There was a fire that surprised her with its intensity. If this fire wasn't reigned in, it would burn her up completely. Along with everything that she knew to be true. "I must be going, Hatter." He nimbly helped her to button her blouse up to her neck. She had only begun to experience how good he was with his hands. She wouldn't soon forget the sensation.

"Of course," he said. "If you need me, I shall be here for you. Always."

"Thank you, Hatter. I'll try to remember that." She swallowed down her swooning heart. "Shall I see you at Margaret's rehearsal dinner?"

He nodded. "I'll await you again, at my shop."

"Would you care to pick me up at my house? It's somewhat of a custom," she nervously droned on, "or, rather, it's something that people do. What I mean to say is that I-"

"Alice?"

"Hm?" she looked up at him.

"I would love to," he smiled sweetly.

Love. The way he spoke the word echoed in the caverns of her mind. It brought images of a castle, a garden, chimneys shaped like rabbit ears, and a vast array of teacups. Snap-dragon-flies with bodies of plum-pudding and wings of holly leaves. If she wasn't mad already, then she would be soon. She was certain of it.

Alice kept recalling the feel of Hatter's body against hers as she lay in her four poster bed, wrapped in her quilt. She couldn't sleep a wink because of it. *Had she been too impulsive? Had she gone and ruined something good? ...Should she have ruined him even more?* She eyed the fabric, the walls, and the small rug at her feet as her lids began to droop. Everything around her was gray. Her home- her world- was so terribly gray. The color that she had grown so used to had suddenly upset her. Maybe painting the walls with varying hues would ease her mind. As she drifted to sleep, she imagined orange, green, purple, blue, earthy brown and warm gold. Those were the right colors, indeed.

"Alice?" A deep and soothing voice floated from her right to left ear. It sounded peculiarly familiar, though she hadn't heard it in a long time. Her eyes opened with a series of blinks. Somehow, the gray had been replaced; there was vibrant color everywhere. An untouched natural landscape stood before her. Daisies danced, roses preened, and tiger-lilies eyed her with fretful contempt. Her search of surroundings stopped at the golden eyes that appeared before her. Those eyes were placed over an impossibly wide smile. Like a mirage, a man appeared behind the features. He had short, fluffy, mauve hair and soft-looking cat ears to match. His darker markings were like a tabby. His style of dress was similar to Hatter's, though his three piece suit was striped in patches of purple, gold, and white. Aside from his off-putting smile and curious eyes, his features were stunning.

The cat man questioned her with concern, "Are you *the* Alice?"

"Of course, I'm Alice." A tail peeked out from behind him to twitch against her face, she brushed it away with a sneeze. "Who else would I be?"

The cat man laughed and retracted his tail. "That sounds like the Alice to me." He retreated, disappearing from sight. To her surprise, he reappeared on a nearby tree branch. "Tell me, Alice, if you look to the left, what do you see?"

A younger Hatter looked startlingly back at her, with a top hat much too large for his head: the same one with a hatband reading, *In this style 10/6.* "Hatter?" Alice asked.

"Alice!" Hatter ran towards her and grasped her hands. "It's so good to see you!"

"What are you doing here, in my dream?" She laughed. "And why are you shorter?"

"The first question is easy: I live here. The second question may require some work: I must be shorter because you are taller." He pushed himself on to his toes, failing to reach her. "Might you lend me some of your height?"

30

Chapter Three:
Of Weddings and Wonder

I n the days of a much taller and older Hatter, the high
council of the White Queen convened. They had
decided that William White Rabbit was the most
responsible for the mission. Theophilus Hatter pouted at
that. **He** was Alice's best friend, after all. The first time they
met was at a tea party. She had sandwiched herself between
a sleeping Silas Dormouse and a grumpy Matias March Hare.

The fact that she was confident enough to take what she
desired made her the most beautiful creature he'd ever seen
in all of Wonderland. Not to mention, her hair was the same
color as the butter he liked on his scones. The wavy strands
danced in the dappled sunlight. But the fringe in her eyes
kept him from fully appreciating the color of her eyes: a well-
brewed tea with speckles of melted honey (his favorite).
"Your hair wants cutting," were his first words to her. He did
so hate it when his hair wandered into his eyes.

She looked at him blankly. "You should learn not to make
personal remarks."

Silas laughed. Matias scoffed. Hatter brought his hands to
his lips, as if to pull his words back. He didn't want her to
think him rude; he needed something clever that would
make her stay. A riddle could work. "Why is a raven like a
writing desk?" he questioned. She'd smiled, then. And he'd

been chasing that smile ever since. His Alice loved riddles. It was too bad that he never had the answers to the ones he made. Yet, she always seemed to come up with something clever for him.

Hatter knew the counsel hadn't voted for him to visit the other realm due to his perceived lack of sanity. *Well, with the way that William White Rabbit obsessed over that pocket watch, they should be doubting **his** sanity!* He may have tricked Alice into following him the first time, but the same act wouldn't work twice. Moreover, William was no fun. It was as if all the colors had drained out of his hair and eyelashes: he drove them away with his schedule-driven stickler attitude. William's red eyes met Theo's with indignation, as if he knew that the hatter was insulting him in his mind. *Maybe he was saying his thoughts aloud? It wouldn't be the first time at council.*

The Duchess stroked her sharp chin in contemplation. "Theophilus Hatter," she stood behind his designated chair at the round table. "You say you have seen *the* Alice in your dream, is that correct?"

"Years ago, Duchess." He looked up at her confusedly. "She looked older- or more beautiful- or older and more beautiful."

"Is that so?" the Duchess smiled knowingly.

"Yes, Duchess. I only say this because the last time she was in our world, we were children together. We were the same height. Or, at least, I was slightly taller."

The regent nodded. "She has aged in her realm, just as we have here. Are you certain that you would know our grown champion upon sight of her?" The Duchess raised a brow. Her face was quite ugly, but her brain was one of the loveliest in Wonderland.

"Absolutely. I would know her anywhere," Hatter affirmed. "I am certain of it."

"He's bonkers!" a guinea pig member of the court yelled in dissent.

"He dreamed her up! There is no Alice!" said a lizard, causing a ruckus.

"Biscuits?" a frog servant stood amidst the hullabaloo and threw said items out to the guests.

That silenced the crowd, which collectively ducked. The Duchess caught her cookie from midair. "Thank you, Melville." She then returned to her speech, "I believe you, Hatter." She delicately placed it onto the plate, offering it in front of him. "That is why I will give you until the turn of the moon. I will set up fitting accommodations for you on the other side." The Duchess smiled. "What do you think of that?"

Theophilus clapped, "I agree! I can't wait to remind Alice about all the fun times we've-"

"No." The Duchess's crooked and gummy smile remained.

"No?" he deflated.

"You must not tell her of Wonderland. She must recall it on her own. Then, she must decide on her own whether our world is worth fighting for. Only at that moment can you both return to save our kingdom."

Hatter was silent. "Our Alice wouldn't forget us," he shook his head before he determinedly looked back at the Duchess. "And she will most definitely be our champion. I know it."

"Excellent, Hatter. That is why I am sending you." She held her hand up to silence the crowd and William White Rabbit's dissent. Her soft expression grew serious. "We are *all* counting on you."

The day dwindled slowly. When the hatter could wait no more, his stride brought him to the front gate of the Everly residence.

"Hatter?" Alice sat on her whitewashed front porch swing. Her hands relinquished a book to the table beside her. "You're early!" She rushed down the steps and opened the latch to greet him with a hug.

After their last encounter he wasn't sure how his Alice felt about him. At first, he was startled by the initiated contact, then overjoyed. He returned her hug with muchness. *Oh, his Alice didn't hate him, after all! Maybe she'd even liked him. Maybe she wanted more?* He didn't dare to dream. He could wait. He'd waited a lifetime and would wait another, for her. He pulled back to look at her face, his hands still on her arms. There were more pressing matters to attend to than his desires, at the moment. "Is there still a rehearsal to attend?"

"I told Margaret everything. She hasn't canceled the wedding. But at least she knows the truth. Even if she's unhappy, she can now make an informed decision." Alice sighed. "I feel bad that it took me so long to tell her."

Hatter's fingers found their way under her chin, prompting her to meet his eyes. "You were only looking out for your sister's happiness. I'm proud of you, Alice. You made the right choice."

"Thank you, Theo. I'm glad that I could count on you for advice."

The hatter's jaw opened and closed as his eyebrows worked through several emotions. "You... recall my name?"

Her eyes searched the walk beneath them as her brows furrowed in concentration. She looked up at him, vindicated, "We're friends. Shouldn't I know? It's Theo- Theophilus- isn't it? I mean unless you've changed it."

He took a deep and shuddering breath in through his nose as her tones caressed his name. He hadn't heard her say it in years. "Yes, Alice. It's Theophilus Hatter. How did you come to know that?"

She played lightly with his lapels, dusting them off. "You told me, silly."

"When?" He searched her face.

Her eyes grew wide at his serious expression. The hatter was never a serious man. The lack of a smile on his face was unnerving. "I don't know, when we met?"

"You're right," he agreed. "Remind me. How long ago was it that we met?"

Alice wondered if the harsh chemicals caused him to forget. "We met at your shop. You should know, you were there."

"Think further."

"Further?" she asked. "Why? Have we met somewhere else? I can't recall a time that I've met you before that."

"You have to." He pleaded, at the end of his rope, and nearly reaching the end of his quest, "Please, Alice, remember..."

"I *can't*." She retreated from his warmth, a look of stubborn concern crossing her face.

"I-" In that moment, he looked truly afraid. Then, as if he'd given up hope. "I'm sorry, Alice. Forgive me."

The two stood in awkward silence for a moment. Alice didn't know how to reassure Theo. Theo was uncertain whether his task would come to a satisfying conclusion. Then, Alice reached out to fold her arm in his. "It's all right. If you say I met you before, then I did. I'm sure that this all has to do with the other world you've been talking about. I'm sorry that I can't remember it. What I *am* certain about is that it's a special place you're hoping to return to soon."

"It is." He nodded. "I am."

Alice squeezed his arm. "Maybe we could talk more about this after the rehearsal dinner?"

"Yes," Hatter swallowed, "of course." They began walking towards the venue downtown.

"My aunt will be there," Alice tried to lighten the mood. "I think you'll like her. She's an eccentric old spinster that lives in an apartment full of cats."

"Cats are fickle creatures," Hatter harrumphed. "Always doing as they please."

"She may be alone, but she's never lonely. She sends me postcards from places all over the world." Alice leaned in towards the hatter, in a whisper, "Still, my mom disagrees and says she's waiting for her prince to come."

"Her prince?" Hatter looked surprised, "Is she royalty? Oh, Alice, are you a princess?" He was awash with excitement. *Princess Alice!* That was something he'd never thought of before.

"Of course not, Hatter," she laughed. "I don't have an ounce of royal blood in me. I'm just an ordinary girl."

"Not ordinary," a knowing look crossed his face, "not in the least."

She was so dazed by the compliment that another man nearly ran into her; his stride taking up the walk. She recognized that sauntering swagger. "Clarence," she deflated. Her neighbor, and family business associate, Clarence Alden had suave locks, an overconfident attitude, and a wallet to match. He would be perfectly pleasing- *perfectly boring*- to some other girl. But was never a thing to her, except an obstacle. His smile simpered as he bowed. "Your mother informed me. I thought we were going to attend your sister's rehearsal dinner together." He stood. "But I see you've opted for the cook instead."

"The hatter, actually," Alice corrected. "He *brilliantly* designed some fascinators for the wedding. Clarence, this is Theo. Theo, this is Clarence." She looked at her other suitor pointedly, "Though I doubt you two will be seeing much of each other."

Clarence provided a fake smile as he walked beside them; or rather, in the middle. "You look like you're getting along like old friends. How long would you two say the two of you have known each other?"

"Oh," she counted the days, "under a month."

"Odd," Clarence said. "That doesn't seem awfully long. And yet, you're nearly walking hand in hand."

"A month!" Hatter's voice was strained as he paid no mind to Clarence's probing statement. "Alice, doesn't the moon make a full turn in a month?"

Clarence looked alarmed. He searched Alice's face with a knowing glance. In that moment she knew he had come to the same conclusion Alice had early on, *this hatter was mad.* But she never cared what the Aldens thought of her, and she wasn't going to start caring now. "If you'll excuse us, Clarence, our hatter has forgotten a certain appointment. He has a remarkably busy schedule, you know. You can keep walking to the venue. We'll see you there."

"Suit yourself," Clarence shrugged, gave one look over his shoulder, and kept his pace in stride.

Alice pulled her date into an alleyway before Clarence could turn around. "Hatter, what is it? What's wrong?"

His back pressed against the cool brick as his mind reeled. "How long is one month, Alice?"

"About thirty days."

"And a day is sunup to sundown?"

She nodded, "Mostly."

"Oh dear," he rested his face in his hands as adrenaline prickled his skin. "Oh my."

"What? What is it?"

"I only have one more day. We only have one more day!" He looked as if he would cry. "It's impossible."

"Perhaps, we can make it possible. I know I said we could talk about it after. But I don't think it can wait. Would it make you feel better if we talk about it now?"

"The White Queen counts six impossibilities before breakfast." He mulled it over, then looked at her. "Is it possible you remember your dream from last night? Is it possible... that I was there?"

"Yes. It is." How could he have known?

"Describe it for me, Alice. What occurred?"

"Well," she swallowed, "you may find it rather odd. It began with a smiling cat-like man who could disappear and reappear."

"Oliver Cheshire," he smiled to himself. "You saw him."

"Then..."

"Yes?"

"There were flowers, living and breathing flowers. And you were there," she breathed out, "as a younger Hatter."

"Is it impossible, Alice," he stalled, "that such a thing actually occurred?"

"How could that be?" She shook her head, "It would have to be years ago for you. It only makes sense as a dream."

"What if I remember that dream, too?"

"What?" she was startled.

"I was there. My 'years ago' was last night to you. I can still recall your pale pink nightgown." Hatter held her hand, placing it gently over his heart. "Alice- am I impossible?" His eyes beseeched her.

"No!" she flushed, "Of course you're not. You're real. I can feel your very heart, warm and beating beneath my fingertips."

"As sure as my heart is beating," his locked eyes with hers, "that place is real. That place is my home. That bloody Red Queen locked up the White Queen and took everything from me, Alice, *everything*. Now there is only you. And if you don't remember, I'll certainly lose you, too." His expression was wavering. "I need you, Alice. We **all** do."

"I don't understand." Alice's face scrunched, "*We?* Do you mean your realm? Your kingdom?"

"You've seen them. You know their faces, if not their names. They all need you. You know that place in your dreams." He leaned forward, "All you have to do is speak its name."

"Dreams?"

"If you dreamt of it last night. You must have thought it was a dream before. A time long ago."

Alice held her head, "I had recurring dreams as a child. Many of us do."

"What were your dreams about?"

"Several mismatched teacups. One boy with rabbit ears and one with mouse ears. They had tails sticking out of their trousers..."

"Yes! You were at Matias March Hare's tea party. He shouldn't like to be called a rabbit, though. He's awfully sensitive about that."

"And there was an awfully pompous caterpillar; he was always asking me who I was."

"He asks that of everybody; he must have a terrible memory. You know who you are. You know where you were. Alice- I need you to say it. Say it for me. *Please*."

Her eyes widened in recollection, "Wonderland."

The hatter's face was overjoyed. "You gave it a bit of your muchness."

"Wonderland," she repeated staunchly. *"You mean Wonderland was- **is**- real?!"*

"Look at me, Alice- you've confirmed that I'm real, haven't you?"

"You! Oh, Hatter!" Her hands roamed his face, "I'd forgotten. I thought it was a dream! Back then, you were just a small boy in an oversized hat. We argued over taking seats, teacups, and riddles: we spent our days making them up and solving them. Why, you introduced me to my favorite tea."

"Jasmine," Hatter said, knowingly.

She removed her hands embarrassedly, "And we, and I-" she stuttered with a blush. She'd kissed her childhood best friend; a friend that she'd thought was imaginary. He'd seen her in her underwear. He'd touched her *intimately.*

"And we...?" Hatter looked confused.

"Nothing," she swallowed. "Now," she started again, "why does Wonderland need my help?"

"The Red Queen seeks to take all of Wonderland from the White Queen by force. The Red Knights, led by the Knave of Hearts, have stolen her and are keeping her locked away somewhere."

"The White Queen? You mean, the young lady with a shawl and bun?" Alice said in foggy recognition.

"Yes. The White Queen ages in reverse. Though she looks youthful, her style is that of an older woman. Soon, she, along with all free life in Wonderland, will be extinguished. That is, unless you can offer us your assistance."

"Me?" Alice pressed a hand to her chest.

"You." He nodded grimly.

"I can't, Hatter," she shook her head. "Look at me! I'm just one ill-equipped person. I mean, I'm currently in a dress and heels! I've never taken on an army, and I'm no strategist. How am I supposed to save her? How am I expected to save a realm? *To save all of Wonderland?* Are you certain that I'm the right Alice for the job?"

"I thought you would say as much. But I believe in you. The White Queen has been given the gift of premonitions. She lives her life in reverse. The queen said that the Alice was the only one that could save her." His hands encompassed hers with a light squeeze. "As far as I'm concerned, there isn't another Alice in the entirety of our worlds. You **are** the Alice: the only one."

"*Theo...*" her eyes searched his face. "But my mother- my sister-"

"Yes. I know. I understand," Theo's hands retracted. "You have family here. That is of utmost importance. Even in Wonderland, I have no such company. The Red Queen took them from me."

"Oh, Theo," she wrapped her arms around him. "I'm so sorry. That sounds like a nightmare." Alice spoke into his shoulder as she held him. "I want to learn everything I can. I want to help. Do you think you can tell me what she has done?"

"Of course, Alice. Sometimes ignorance is not bliss." He gave a choked whisper, "My family were messengers for the White King, whose assassination caused the war. Some members of my family were killed, while others were locked up. Some of them have gone into hiding in faraway kingdoms. As you can see, I have no choice but to fight; my family cannot rest until the Red Queen is vanquished."

"I see." Alice was silent for a moment. "We wouldn't be able to come back to this world- my world- would we?"

"No." He cast his eyes solemnly to the ground. "I'm not certain that we would."

"I... need some time. We have one more day." Alice held Hatter closer, for fear of knowing her choice could cost her him or her family. Neither choice felt acceptable: it was another impossibility. "Don't we?"

A sorrowful distance filled his eyes, "One more day, Alice." His hand smoothed over her hair. "Only then can you decide what's worth fighting for."

It was the day of Margaret's wedding. As she was practicing her vows, Alice was wondering whether to make her own vows to serve the White Queen. It was a lot like an arranged marriage, having been chosen to serve a kingdom. *Were there any benefits to such an arrangement?* In her mind's eye, she saw Theo. If she were to spend her life in another world, he could possibly be her only companion. *While she enjoyed spending time with him, did she want to spend her life with him? Did she want a war to make that choice for her?*

But she was only thinking of herself in that moment- of her own wants and needs. What did Theo think of her? Would he want to spend a lifetime by her side? Would she be odd as the only human in Wonderland? Was Hatter swayed by her amorous intentions? She'd practically thrown herself at him the other day. Alice noticed how standoffish Hatter was when he picked her up for the rehearsal dinner. He must have still been feeling awkward about the whole situation. Plus, their first date had been muddied by inner turmoil about saving Wonderland. She couldn't sleep a wink because of it. Alice wondered: did Hatter truly like her as more than a friend, or were his actions solely to get her to return with him? She sighed. He had told her she was full of muchness, but she could feel none of it at all.

Margaret took a seat beside her on the velvet chaise. "You look as pale and blue as your bridesmaid dress." She laughed lightly.

Alice stepped out of her mind to truly look at her sister. This may be one of the last days she saw her. She put the image of her sister in a wedding gown to mind. It should be the happiest day of her life. Alice hoped it would be.

"You know," said Margaret, "they say that the color of a gown will influence your future. If that's so, then your love will come true."

"Love?" Alice turned, "Me? Who said anything about *my* love life? Today is all about you. You're the one who is walking down the aisle."

Margaret smiled. "And yet, much like me, you have the look of a girl about to make a choice. Love is a dangerous and wonderful thing. I could see the sparks of it from your seat at my rehearsal dinner."

Alice played coy, "I have no idea what you're talking about."

Her sister smiled. "Love can sometimes take the opposite seat of reason. We can use Luke as an example. I knew he was a flirt when I first met him. It's always been a part of who he is. Other than that, he is a very attentive and loving man with a respectable job. He makes me laugh, and he will provide a safe home. He'd make a good father. I can't bring myself to throw that away for something he does in jest. I mean, I have to trust that he would never *truly* leave me for someone else. If I didn't trust that, then I couldn't marry him."

A look of concern flashed over Alice's face.

"I'm ready to stand by him through the good times and the bad, because that's what marriage is."

"But, you don't have to stand by him!" Alice clasped her sister's hands. "You still have time. I'll dissent to the marriage at the altar, and we can-"

"Alice," her sister closed her eyes, "you may not agree with my decision, but I am grateful that you allowed me the choice. I know this is the right one for me. You see, there are people in this world we can't help but love. We cannot choose them any more than we can change them. We can only support our loved one's endeavors... Even if their choices take them on a difficult journey."

"...I see," Alice murmured.

"Will you support me, Alice?" asked her sister.

"Of course!" Alice said.

"That means the world to me." She looked every bit as perfect as Alice had known her, with a fitted bodice swimming in a full skirt of tulle, silk, and lace. Her veil framed her softly smiling face. "I know I will support you in all of your endeavors, as well."

Alice nodded contentedly. "Thank you, Margaret. I wish you all the happiness in the world."

"Likewise." Margaret stalled. "You know, your dress and fascinator were supposed to be navy like all the other bridesmaids, but the hatter insisted that this powder blue was your only color. He's such an odd fellow. But he was right."

Hatter watched as Alice grinned and danced along with her sister at the reception. He wondered if he had seen her smile like that before, or if he could ever make her smile like that again. He wondered if he could tear her away from the people that made her smile. Alice had a sister. She had a mother. She had an aunt that liked cats.

Feline friends didn't talk in her world. He'd found out after several attempts at conversation. It took a while for him to make that conclusion because cats could be snobbish conversation partners, after all. Alice liked her world. She wouldn't want to leave it for a childhood place she barely remembered visiting. *Why would she risk her life for people she didn't know or love? Why would she spend her days in a world that she had dismissed and deemed nothing but a dream?*

He'd decided: she wouldn't. She couldn't. From her spot on the dancefloor, her smile warmed the room. Yet it failed to lighten the heavy burden on his heart. He didn't want to make her leave such a peaceful world. He watched her dance as a melancholy feeling settled into the pit of his stomach. He wished he were in the mood to dance. He wished he could sway with her to the music of Wonderland.

He wanted her to listen to instruments she'd never seen before and teach her his favorite steps. He wanted to share his customs: the feasts and festivals. He wanted to see her shock and awe and enjoyment as she learned new things. He wanted to see her grow to find it all to be so commonplace-take it for granted- as he had. He wanted to see her feeling at home in his home. Such extreme happiness wasn't meant to be. At least he had done all he could. He would protect her cherished life. He would find a way to save the White Queen and Wonderland on his own.

"A lovely ceremony," Hatter met Alice with a weak smile as she returned to their numbered guest table. "May Margaret's choices bring her ever-happiness."

"I hope so," Alice sipped her drink and caught her breath. "I really do."

There was a heavy silence between them. The sun was going down and Hatter would soon be gone with it. Whether or not Alice would go with him remained her decision. A decision- it appeared to the hatter- she'd already made. He stood from the table, patting his top hat onto his wild curls.

"Margaret and Luke haven't cut the cake yet. Aren't you having a slice?"

"No, thank you," he tipped the brim of his hat in dissent.

She placed her glass on the table, "Then, would you like to dance? I haven't seen you on the dancefloor all evening. As I recall, you're rather good. Maybe you could teach me a thing or two?"

An image came to his mind's eye of twirling a young Alice in a field of daisies as Matias March Hare played the fiddle and Silas Dormouse clapped along. He shook it off. Those were only memories now. "Alice..." He paused to build a shrine for her in his mind. He could worship there after she'd gone from his life. "My Alice. I must be going."

"So soon?"

"Time is calling me home." He pressed a hand to his chest. "I can feel it in my ticker."

She stood. "But we don't have a plan..."

"A plan?" Hatter's alarm became a hushed tone, "The only plan I've ever had in my life was you. Without you by my side, I'm not sure what will happen to Wonderland. I'm not sure what will happen," his voice became impossibly smaller as he searched her eyes, "to me."

Alice watched his pale throat bob. "To you?"

"*I love you*, Alice Everly," Hatter said as he took her hand. "I've loved you since the first moment you put me in my place and stole my teacup. You were the answer to all my riddles, spoken and unspoken. And If this is the last time I see you, then I'm glad I was able to tell you so."

Alice could only stare with her mouth agape.

"Now, unfortunately," the hatter continued, "I must go. Fair fairing, Alice."

"Wait!" Alice wouldn't let go of his hand. "You... love me?"

He gave a faint smile. "With all that I am."

"Love, as in really and truly *love*? That kind of love?"

"I would give you as many 'loves' as you'd like."

Alice moved forward, "And you'd never grow tired of me if I were- or possibly will be- the only woman in Wonderland?"

"Never."

"Even if I were frustrated or couldn't understand-"

"Alice."

"If I couldn't memorize the words and holidays, or properly cook traditional-"

"*Alice*," Hatter smiled, "never is an **awfully** long time."

She looked at him in silence for a long moment before grasping his lapels, "Then, don't you *dare* leave me behind."

Chapter Four:
Of Quests and Companions

Alice placed a kiss on her sister's cheek and then her mother's. She held them tightly in her last moments before she spied the groom. "You had better uphold your promise to make my sister happy," she leveled with Luke, "or, so help me, I'll make it so that you never feel *inspired* to flirt again."

Luke swallowed. "I will. Cross my heart."

Margaret said fondly to Alice, "I hope you and your friend find happiness as well."

"Margaret!" Alice said.

"As long as Alice is there," Hatter nodded, "my happiness is assured."

Alice's mother raised a brow as she placed down her drink.

"Come on, Theo," Alice pushed through the embarrassment, "let's be on our way."

After bidding a good night- and a silent farewell- to her family, Hatter and Alice ran to the house in the woods just as the moon was rising. The cuckoo clocks on the wall, which were winding counterclockwise, had just begun to chime. The mortar holding up the walls was beginning to crumble onto the sofas by the fireplace.

"This is impossible!" Alice ducked. "How can we find the rabbit hole? Is there another entrance to Wonderland hidden somewhere in here?" Alice's adrenaline began to spike as she stepped aside to avoid falling lumber.

"Nothing is impossible. This way," Hatter removed a drop cloth covering an ornate antique-looking mirror. Sparrows were carved in each corner of the dark wooden frame.

"Is this a metaphor?" Alice asked as she confusedly eyed her reflection in the looking-glass.

"I haven't the slightest idea what a 'meta' is for, Alice. The White Queen will know." He brought his hand up to the glass. Alice's eyes widened as Hatter's fingers sunk into the mirror like it were a pool of water. He smiled at her wonder. "After you." It was as if he were holding an invisible door open for her.

Curiouser and curiouser, Alice thought as she was able to poke her head through the flat object without resistance. On the other side of the glass was a well-maintained courtyard. Stark white magnolia blossoms stood out against dark green shrubbery. Light colored stones dotted the ground in a chessboard pattern, leading to a center circle before the white castle that resembled the dark and light of yin and yang. She tried to take her head out to comment on the beauty of the place to Hatter but was stuck. The mirror only allowed her to travel one way.

Alice's heart sped up rapidly at that realization. Fear gripped her as she wondered if she would be trapped between worlds for all eternity. When she felt Hatter's fingers entwine with her own on the other side, she knew that everything would be all right. She would be safe with Theo. Alice found the strength to pull herself completely through the looking-glass as the hatter followed at her heels.

When she turned around to help him out, the mirror was gone.

The couple had arrived among a row of magnolias when the Duchess and her troops approached. It was only when the old Duchess' thin lips gave a knowing smile that Alice realized she was still holding Hatter's hand. She dropped it swiftly, unaware if she was breaking customs. "My Duchess," Alice curtsied as she recognized the ugly face and warm heart before her. Theo followed suit with a bow.

"Arise, Fair Champion," the Duchess spoke sweetly. "Do you know why you are here?"

Alice stood. "To save the White Queen." She winced in trepidation, "Though, to be perfectly honest, I have no idea how. Do we know the specifics?"

"Are you sure that's **the** Alice?" Matias March Hare stepped forward.

He looked a year older than Theo, with the tall, furry, brown ears of a hare. Alice could see the pink in the center and wanted to rub them between her thumb and forefinger. Matias' styled dark locks were tossed around them. The man had shrewd bespectacled eyes and a tan wool suit. *Perhaps all of the men in Wonderland were curiously handsome; each in their own way*, Alice noted. Hatter always said that he was mad, but only in the angry sense of the word: he had the mind of a brilliant scholar.

"If she *were* the Alice, wouldn't she know how to save our queen?"

Before Alice could answer for herself, she felt Hatter's strong hand offering support on her shoulder. "There could never be another Alice."

Matias was taken aback at his friend's declaration.

"The White Queen's premonition was limited, and information was only provided to the Duchess beforehand. There's no way Alice could have known," Hatter concluded.

The Duchess's thin lips quirked once more. She had chosen well to send Theophilus instead of William. "Alice," she directed her speech, "you, alone, have been entrusted to retrieve the White Queen from the Red Castle. I warn you, it will be dangerous, but we must trust in the White Queen's prophecy. You were the way she foresaw balance being restored to Wonderland."

Alice felt a flip in her stomach. "I'm sorry- did you say, *alone?*"

"Alone," echoed the Duchess.

"I volunteer to assist Alice in her endeavors." Hatter kept his hand firmly planted on her person. Which was a good idea, because she felt like she was going to faint under the ambiguity and responsibility of her mission.

"I'm afraid that was not part of the premonition," spoke the Duchess as she stroked her sharp chin. "I suppose you may travel with her as a guide, but your fate will be uncertain. All that can be assured is that Alice alone will be the one to meet the White Queen in the castle. After that, events are unknown."

"Then, I will lead her to the Red Castle Keep and stay by her side until the very last moment. Who will join me to support our champion?"

"I will," Matias stepped forward as he looked Alice over. "After all, someone should keep an eye on our imposter."

Alice dissented, "If you can find me an Alice who would like to sacrifice herself in my stead, then be my guest."

Matias snorted.

Silas Dormouse stretched out his arms sleepily. "I guess I should tag along as well," he yawned. The mouse man looked two years younger than Alice, with soft blueish hair topped by velvet soft, thin, round ears. His large eyes were a downturned gray with long light lashes. His clothing was a more relaxed poet's shirt and light woolen breeches. It was then that she noticed a pink tail peeking through. At the sight of it, she remembered that Matias had a fluffy rabbit-like tail. Alice fought back a laugh that such an uptight man could have such a soft looking appendage.

Hatter's friends had gathered to support him. Well, by transitive property, to support them both. Alice looked up at the hatter. He had offered himself to an uncertain fate to better protect her. She felt a curiosity and awe swirling inside of her. "The Red Queen is a murderer and a tyrant," Alice began as she took him aside. "She has harmed those you care for deeply. How can you offer to deliver yourself to the most dangerous place in all of Wonderland? How can you find the strength to fight back? Shouldn't you stay here, safe with the Duchess in the White Castle walls, until the prophecy is fulfilled?"

"I'm pleased to know that you care about my wellbeing, Alice," Hatter held her hand in his own. "But, I don't do well with waiting; not when there's so much doing to be done. Besides, my confidence is not in myself. It lies in you. You're my strength: the little Alice that lives inside of my heart. I trust that you'll be able to see us all through."

"What if I let you down?" her eyes sought his own.

"You could never let me down," he smiled. "Half the battle is already won because you're here with me in Wonderland. We just have another half of the battle to go. That doesn't seem so bad, now, does it?"

She looked into the hopeful eyes of the hatter and, for the first time, felt a muchness growing about her. "Let's just hope this second half goes more smoothly than the first one."

Silas, Matias, and Theo gathered supplies and headed out the gates of the White Queen's Kingdom into disputed territory. They walked through the wide-open plains where the land was flat, bleak, and grassy. Trees appeared to loom on the horizon as they soon transitioned into a dark and densely-wooded forest where no birds could be heard and no animals seen.

Alice was about to ask about the local flora and fauna, but decided against it. She'd rather not know what type of doom awaited her up in the trees. What she had come to know was that the eerie Whispering Woods was called that because the trees spoke when the wind was strong enough to whistle through them. Some said the trees told the secrets of those who passed through. On the other side of the forest was the Red Queen's stolen part of Wonderland. The trek through the forest avoided the main cobblestone path through the plains which was guarded heavily by Red Knights. The surreptitious trek was supposed to take a night. Though the journey felt longer under the interrogation of Hatter's friend.

"Who are you, really?" Matias asked Alice. "What benefit do you seek from offering your assistance to our kingdom? Or, do you just have a savior complex? Do you have a praise kink and want to be lauded as a hero?"

"Matias," said Hatter, "your questioning is nearly as circular as our path."

"Hatter's right, you know. You sound like that caterpillar, always asking me who I am. Did he retire and have you taken his place?" Alice asked. The phrase 'jumping mad' came to mind as she considered the man's hare-like appearance.

"Perhaps," Matias gave a self-assured smile.

Alice sighed. "For the thousandth time, I'm Alice- **the** Alice, all right? And I get the feeling I've done something to make you dislike me. You wish she was someone else, but I'm the only one that showed up. So, we're going to have to get along."

"Don't worry. It's not just you, Alice. I don't think he's ever liked anyone," Silas snickered.

"Why do you say that?" Matias stopped to cross his arms.

Alice stopped as well, to pointedly press a finger to his chest. "You were mad at me in childhood, ever since I showed up to your tea party uninvited! Well, I'm sorry that I didn't get the invitation all the way in another realm. But I have a feeling, if I lived here, I wouldn't have been invited either."

"That's right. Who invited you to my tea party, anyway? You party crasher."

"*Don't blame me!* I was invited by a boy with cat ears and a wide smile." Alice put her hands atop her head in emphasis. "He showed me the way."

"Oliver," Matias rolled his eyes in exasperation.

Alice had an inkling she wasn't the only stranger to show up to one of Matias' tea parties under Oliver Cheshire's invitation. "Where is he now?" she questioned, "I haven't seen him since my dream."

"Were you dreaming about Oliver again?" Hatter joined the group in their pause. "When?"

"Come on," urged Matias, "we can't stand here dawdling. We have more ground to cover before moon-up."

"Just the other night," Alice answered, "when he was pointing me to a younger you."

"I see. No one has seen him around since the Red Queen took power," Hatter's said. "We all were wondering if he's all right. But, then again, maybe he found a particularly nice place to nap and doesn't want Silas to steal it from him."

"Well," Alice offered, "I wouldn't worry. It was just a dream of mine."

"Nothing is ever just a dream," Silas said sleepily. "Especially in Wonderland; we're so close to Dreamland. Why do you think I spend most of the time with my eyes closed?"

"What do you mean?" Alice asked.

"Dreamland is the realm that borders on Wonderland," said Silas. "You can visit it by foot, or by a quick snooze. I should say I'm a rather successful entrepreneur there. Since you're from another world, I should warn you: our dreams have meaning. Some have a life of their own."

"I'll keep that in mind," said Alice. "Could it be that Oliver relocated to the safety of Dreamland?"

"Perhaps," Hatter nodded as they continued on.

"We still have a journey ahead of us," sighed Matias, "and the ground is stretching far faster than our feet can travel."

"Well that pessimistic outlook won't get us anywhere," said Alice.

"Not pessimistic;" said Matias, "it's a logical outlook. Stand still and look," he directed, prompting her gaze.

She eyed him suspiciously before checking the ground. A rock she was staring at seemed to travel as if it were on a conveyor belt. *"Curiouser and curiouser,"* she remarked with wide eyes. "Is the path changing due to the Red Queen's magic?"

"Highly likely. We have entered her territory, and she likes to make it difficult for her enemies. Most get tired of walking and turn around," said Silas. "Or they take the paved road and run into the guards."

The companions wandered up and down a corkscrew path, trying turn after turn, yet always ending back at the same gnarly old oak tree. Alice breathed from exertion and wiped the sweat from her brow. "In my world, we'd be across the length of this forest by now."

"We aren't in your world, are we?" said Matias. "You'll do well to remember that."

Alice stuck out her tongue.

"In Wonderland, if you want to get somewhere else, you have to travel at least twice as far," Hatter said. "Which means we're halfway there."

"I guess that makes sense," Alice agreed.

Matias took a seat on the ground. "We'll settle here for the night."

"But we've just had lunch and the sun is still high in the sky," said Alice.

"That was supper," corrected Silas.

"High in the sky, night is nigh," offered Hatter.

"It helps the little ones to remember that rhyme," Matias smirked as he looked down his nose at Alice.

"Oh." Her heart burned. She was beginning to understand why Hatter was so confused in her world. "Well, I'm decidedly un-little."

"For now," Matias assented.

Theo took Alice's hand with a warm smile. "We have days and nights: two or three at a time. In the winter, we can have as many as five nights strung together- to conserve the warmth. I know you'll get the hang of it, Alice."

She sure hoped so, if her future life depended on it. "Are five nights warmer than one?"

"Yes. Five times as warm, if you have the right partner."

"Oh," a heat came to her ears. "I see." No sooner than she took a seat on the ground had all the light gone out of the sky.

She clutched onto Theo's arm at the sudden change, suddenly feeling like a child in the dark. He comforted her with a reassuring squeeze of her hand. Alice smiled. "I'm sorry. I wasn't expecting things to change so quickly."

"Neither was I," Hatter said softly.

She knew he wasn't talking about the evening. She hadn't expected her feelings about Theo to progress so quickly, but he had always been dear to her. He had told her he loved her. She didn't know if her feelings were love, having never been in love before. *Could this be what it felt like?* As she looked from his sweet face up to the sparkling sky, she noticed something peculiar. "Wait a minute," she pointed upwards. "Is that the constellation of Orion? Isn't he standing backwards?"

"It's right ways around for Wonderland," Hatter whispered as his friends unrolled the sleeping bags from their packs and settled in for the night. "It all depends on which way you look at it."

"How curious," Alice yawned.

"Get some sleep, Alice," Hatter said. "I'll take the first watch."

"But I'm not sleepy."

He laid out her bed next to him. "You will be. The forest knows you need your rest." He took his seat, propped against the old tree. Alice settled under the covers and laid her head onto Hatter's lap. In a strange world, full of even stranger strangers, he made her feel at home. She closed her eyes. She didn't have to search long for sleep. With the way he brushed a hand over her crown while humming an oddly familiar tune, she was out like a light.

Alice felt kisses along her neck that stirred her from her sleep. "*Ah*," she breathed out in pleasure as a thumb brushed over the fabric clothing her nipple.

"*Shh*," Theo whispered beside her ear; his voice was warm and rough, "you don't want them to hear us, do you?"

She didn't know what possessed the hatter to become so bold, but she didn't mind it either.

"I've wanted to do this since the moment I saw you in Otherland."

"Have you?" She cupped his face to examine his wanting features in the full moonlight. "I'm glad you told me. I must admit, I haven't been able to shake that feeling either."

"We might not survive this journey- the Red Queen will make sure of it if she can. I don't want to die without tasting you," he said in a hushed voice. "Will you allow me the pleasure of having you, if only for tonight?" His eyes swept over her. "My Alice..."

She searched his eyes before nodding shyly. She didn't know what had come over her, but he was right. This might be the only opportunity they had. The blood thrumming between her legs had left her brain. She'd finally become as mad as the hatter. Her lips met his in a heated kiss. He gasped into her mouth as she gripped his manhood through the fabric of his pants. He was hard as he pressed into her. His shape fit her palm nicely as she moved her hand up slowly and down. "You didn't think you'd be the only one having fun, did you?"

"Alice," his hips ground against her hand, creating much needed friction. "You'll drive me sane if you don't let me taste you."

She laughed against his lips with another kiss. His tongue teased hers as he let out the sweet soft noises she'd heard only once, at his house in the woods.

His hand moved expertly down, undoing the front buttons of her dress. Her breasts came free of the built-in bra, nipples pebbled by the cool night air. But they weren't cold for long, as the hatter teased them between his lips, tongue, and teeth. When he began to suck, Alice's back arched into the sensation. A wave of pleasure crashed over her, causing her to tighten her thighs around the hatter's hand which had slipped up and under her gown, teasing her swollen entrance through her undergarments.

"You're all wet, Alice," the hatter whispered. "Naughty. Is it just for me?"

"All for you," Alice bucked into his touch as he slipped a finger under the fabric and caressed her. In time, he entered between her folds.

"My Alice," the hatter kissed her clavicle and throat. "All mine."

She had to bite her lip to stifle her moan as his fingers expertly played her. The way he was sucking on her chest and gently pumping his digits into her as his thumb toyed with her clit had her heart racing. She could hear it in her ears. She needed more. "I want you," she said between breaths. "I want you inside me, Theo."

He gave a soft smile as he looked up at her. "Are you certain?"

"Now. Here."

He released her breast with a sweet sound and unbuttoned his pants to withdraw himself. Alice ran her hands over the length of him, causing Theo's head to roll back as his body shivered with desire. When they locked eyes again, Alice stood and stepped out of her underwear before bracing against the tree. She turned to look at the hatter from over her shoulder. He paused to observe the curvature of her back and her slick entrance. Unable to bring himself away, he knelt to lick her and paused to suck on her exposed clit. She pressed into the sensation, breathy gasps escaping her as her legs grew shaky from standing.

"No fair!" She reminded him, "I want you, Theo. I don't want to cum without you inside of me."

"My Alice is spoiled." Theo stood and brushed his face with the back of his hand before gently steadying her waist. "Are you ready for me?"

She nodded eagerly.

"Good girl," he easily slid into her from behind. "So good for me... *Ah.*" Alice echoed the noise of pleasure. He fit her perfectly. Her walls clenched at the sensation of him inside of her. "I'm going to move." He pressed in and out, creating a humming warmth in her body. Hatter's hands moved down and over her breasts, teasing her nipples as he entered and exited, hips snapping against her body. She was climbing higher towards her peak.

"I want to see you when you cum for me;" he breathed, "I want to kiss your lips."

"Yes," she hastily agreed as she gripped the tree.

He pulled himself out and turned her around so her back was flush against the bark. He took a moment to explore her mouth and chest with his lips and tongue before wrapping his arms under her legs and lifting her up. "Is this all right?" he asked.

She nodded, eagerly guiding him into her once more. They sighed into each other as the hatter again picked up speed. "It feels so good," Alice toyed with herself as the hatter pressed on. Her other arm was around his strong neck and back for support. He held her fast; she was certain he'd never let her go, even once he'd spilled himself inside of her.

"So good, Alice," Theo's head came to rest on her shoulder as he moved in and out.

"Keep going," Alice breathed as her legs tightened around his waist, the sensation of him echoing inside of her. "Just like that. Yes." She could feel herself getting there. "I want you to cum inside me, cum with me."

"Alice..." his voice became something of a whine.

"*Ah!*" Sparks exploded and flickered behind her eyelids as she came undone on the hatter's cock. Her body desperately tried to pull him in, deeper and deeper, into her depths. She whimpered the feeling against the hatter's shoulder.

His guiding hand brought her face to his in a kiss as his other arm tightened its grip on her waist, pulling her impossibly closer. He gave a silent moan of pleasure against her lips as his warm seed pumped inside of her, seeping out and around her entrance and his member.

When she came back down from her high, Alice's eyes and ears opened to the snores of her companions. She looked up at the hatter's sleeping face and, for a moment, was disappointed: it was only a dream. But she'd never had such a dream about him before. How curious that the first time she did it would be from sleeping on his lap. It felt so real; she could still feel the arousal slick between her legs. She wondered, in a melancholy way, if her dream would ever come true: if they could both make it out of the ordeal intact. For a second she wondered if she should wake him and make it come true. After seeing Silas' awake and knowing smile she embarrassedly covered her face with her blanket and went back to sleep.

Chapter Five:
Of Bonds and Blunders

The moon fell as Alice dozed. Soon the sun filled the sky once more. Upon waking, Alice found herself sprawled across Hatter's chest and body. His face was peaceful, and heavy with sleep. Recalling her dream, she pulled herself away in swift shyness. The movement caused his eyelids to flutter open. A smile came across his face as he felt her missing warmth and sat up to greet her, "Good 'morrow, Alice."

"Good 'morrow," she replied in turn. She couldn't bring herself to tear her eyes away from the golden flecks in his own, as if they were an answer to an unspoken riddle.

"We're still here," Matias sat with his arms and legs crossed. Silas was sleeping, curled in on his hands. "Something happened between you two in Otherland, didn't it?"

"Otherland?" asked Alice. She'd heard that word in her dream.

"Your world," offered Hatter, softly.

"Right," Alice nodded.

"And while the queen is not around, no less. Have you told the Duchess of your courtship?" Matias inclined.

"Mati..." Hatter mollified.

"What's wrong with a kiss?" Alice said. "Does it, or any other act, have to lead to courtship?"

Matias inhaled sharply, which caused Silas to do the same. Awakening, the young mouse man opened one eye. "You *kissed* the Alice?"

"I should say that she kissed me." A warm flush spilled across the bridge of his nose and ears.

Matias growled, "Do friends do that in Otherland, Alice? What were your intentions?"

"Matias!" Hatter warned.

"Who knows! Why should we have to explain ourselves to you or your queen?" Alice asked.

"You answer my questions with more questions, False Alice-"

"False?!"

"-so, I shall do the same." The hare man leaned forward. "Why should you live in a world in which you don't follow the customs? Do you know what that one kiss signifies to Hatter? To all of us?"

"*Enough!*" Hatter stood. "Alice is here to save our kingdom. That is her purpose here, and her one purpose only. We are her tools, for her to use as she deems fit."

"Oh, she'll use you, all right." Matias sat back on his haunches.

"*And I wouldn't mind!*" Hatter shook with unshed emotion.

Silas blinked up at him with empathy.

Alice grasped Theo's hand. "Hatter, I would never use you." She looked to her companions sternly, "I would never use any of you. I'm sorry if things we've done are considered unacceptable here, but they were acceptable in Otherland. We should come to understand and support one another's customs. Although, I'm still not sure about what a kiss signifies in Wonderland."

"A bond," Matias offered.

"A bond?" Alice repeated.

"A contract, so to speak, to be committed to one another," added Silas.

"If a contract is made by kissing, then I assume two people must be betrothed before sleeping together," Alice proposed.

"Not at all," Silas smiled. "That's a far less serious offense to the citizens of Wonderland. Sex is not a bond between a mated pair but considered recreation between any consenting parties."

This world really was a backwards world if a kiss meant more than sex. But she needed to abide by Wonderland's customs. "I see," Alice nodded. "I will be more careful not to form contracts with anyone from now on. Though, I can promise that I will do my best to keep Theo safe."

Hatter's brows moved upwards.

"Good," Matias nodded. "The contract is invalid because, as you said, it occurred outside of our realm. Further, the queen did not sanction it. Shall we forget this ordeal ever happened and move on with our task?"

"I still don't see why the queen should be involved," Alice huffed. "But I can see that it would be rude for an outsider to question your customs."

"Quite," said Matias.

Alice reluctantly untangled her hand from Theo's. "If forgetting our past involvement is appropriate, then so be it."

Hatter didn't want to forget. *Never.* No, not at all.

The Red Queen's Kingdom was made up of little brooks running across the countryside. The ground was divided into a checkered pattern by hedges, going brook to brook. Black briars stood in stark contrast to specks of white swamp roses. The chessboard theme had continued from the White Queen's Kingdom. Which made sense because it was all her kingdom at one point. Avoiding the paved path, traversing the small bodies of water and tall grass made traveling difficult.

After what felt like hours of walking to the Red Castle in the distance, they had finally approached the thorny crimson rose hedges of the queen's garden. Alice regretfully recalled painting the petals red and how they pricked at her fingers. They were still the same dreadful color of her blood mixing with acrylic. The war between white and red kingdoms had truly been a long and terrible one, if it continued from her childhood.

The group scoped out the tall black iron gate that surrounded the property. There were no weak points apart from the entrance, where two guards stood. Alice jumped up on the slippery poles, but they cast her back down. They could have been oiled; or maybe inanimate objects just didn't take a liking to her. "We need to find a way in," she turned to her companions to hatch a plan.

"*You* need to find a way in," Matias corrected. "This was as far as we were able to take you, remember?"

"Fine," Alice said. "*I* need to find a way in. Does anyone have suggestions?"

Silas rummaged through his pocket. "I was saving this for a nap in a teakettle later. But you can have it, Alice."

She held the vial in her hands. "*Drink Me*," she read aloud. She remembered once she had. It made her small. But how was it she became tall again? *Oh, yes.* "Do we have any *Eat Me* cake?"

Everyone's pockets turned up empty.

"I know the recipe, and I can bake it up quickly. The Red Queen hardly goes into the kitchens when she has servants to cook for her," Hatter affirmed. "Perhaps I can hand it to you from the inside."

"I don't know if that's the best plan, Hatter," said Silas. "There's no way you'll be able to sneak past her security unnoticed."

"Has a kiss from Alice gone and made you even madder?" Matias crossed his arms.

"For once, Matias is right," Alice frowned. "You'd be handing yourself to the enemy."

"If I were in the castle, I could be by your side- I could further assist you with your mission," Hatter appeased. "I don't like the idea of you going in to face the Blood Queen on your own."

"She has taken your family captive in the past. She wouldn't miss the opportunity to lock you up. Or even worse, to eliminate you all together. I don't like this plan," Alice shook her head.

Hatter held her hand in his own. "We don't have any others."

Matias sighed. "It looks like we will have to work on getting Theophilus back out safely. Silas and I will take care of it. Don't worry about him, Alice. Then again, I don't need to tell *you* that."

"Right. What exactly is your problem?" Alice pointedly stomped over. "I'm doing the best I can with the information I've got. Yet, you've held a grudge against me since day one. There isn't one single thing that I could do to make you like me, now, is there?"

"I'm afraid that's what he's angry about," offered Hatter.

"*Hatter*," the hare grit out.

"He has to like you; it's in his blood."

66

"What?" Alice pulled back, surprised.

"He wants to hate you, but he can't," Silas said.

"You're the one true savior- *the Alice*- deemed so by the White Queen," Hatter confirmed.

"She doesn't need to know the details!" Matias interrupted.

"It would be helpful if she does." Hatter continued, "The White Queen bestowed some power upon you with that premonition. Those that swore a blood allegiance to her kingdom are under her influence. They are sworn to protect and serve you."

"I don't understand," Alice spoke distantly.

"It's a magic contract woven in our blood," Silas rolled up his unbuttoned shirt sleeves. She could see the brief flicker of a golden spark of magic when he pointed to his veins.

Alice looked on in awe. "Your realm really is reliant on contracts, isn't it?" She then turned with new awareness to her Hatter. *Did that mean the way he felt about her- that kiss and all that desire- was only inspired by some spell?*

Suddenly, a guard called from nearby, "I hear voices!"

"Go on! We'll distract them," Silas pulled Matias back into the Whispering Woods to make scattered noises, throwing branches and stones in differing directions.

"Hatter," Alice breathed, "I'm scared."

"Drink, Alice. I won't let them lay a hand on you, not while I'm around."

"No. I'm not scared of them." She declined the potion with her hand. "I've dealt with the Queen of Hearts before. What I'm afraid of is losing you, my best friend, all over again. *For good.*"

Hatter turned to see the Red Knights with cloaks numbered like cards running after Silas and Matias towards the forest. They didn't have the time to stall any longer.

"Forgive me, Alice, I know you aren't favorable to this realm's contracts; but I, for one, don't want to break our accord." He took the vial from her hands, tore the cork out with his teeth, took the potion in his mouth, and imparted a kiss to press it past her lips.

She swallowed and sputtered to take a breath. She brushed the droplets from her lips as she began to feel a curious sensation. "Hatter?" Alice blinked and looked down at her hands as she felt herself shrinking.

"You'll never lose me Alice." He watched her fall into her large clothing as he took the lavender handkerchief out from his breast pocket, enough to cover her figure. He leaned down after she'd wrapped herself in the fabric. "Never." He stuffed her larger dress into his hat for safe keeping. Hatter felt the heat rise in his cheeks as he paused to blush at her underwear before stuffing that into his hat as well. "I'll meet you on the other side."

She couldn't help but hope for another meaning from his words. "Promise?" her whelming tears felt too large for her face.

"I promise. Now, don't go flooding all of Wonderland for me. I haven't found the time to learn how to swim," he teased in farewell.

Alice watched from a safe perch, inside of the fence, as her best friend- and something more- disappeared behind a row of thorns. She wondered if, or how, he would make it inside and evade the guards. As she turned around to gauge the distance, she saw how the trimmed and tidy grass seemed like a sprawling forest before her. She sighed. It seemed like

Wonderland was full of forests; she'd only made her way through one the day before.

Alice jumped down from the fence and convinced her feet to continue walking. She looked up to see where the sun was in the sky to gauge the time of day. Just as she shielded her eyes, a smile like a crescent moon appeared on the horizon. *Had night arrived again?* It was then followed by two calm yellow eyes and a familiar set of cat ears tucked into mauve hair. "Oliver!" Alice said as she observed the cat man floating above her.

"Please," he said, "call me Chesh. You always used to. What are you doing down there, little mouse?"

"I'm still a human- at least I still think I am- and I'm headed into the castle. What are you doing here? Hatter and his friends say they haven't seen you for ages."

"Ah. But are you so certain that you've seen me?"

"I'm not so certain of anything, any longer. You and this whole world may as well be a figment of my imagination."

"Hm." The cat man turned to float on his back. "You have quite the imagination."

"Well," Alice said as she tiredly leapt over a fallen acorn, "I guess I do, if I've decided to believe in myself."

"A wise choice. How can you believe in anything if you don't believe in yourself?"

"You're right. I don't suppose you could imagine offering me some help?"

"Couldn't possibly," his smile grew wider. "Could probably."

Alice rolled her eyes. The roundabout way of speech in Wonderland would take some getting used to. Being direct and forward was in her and Hatter's best interest right now. "Would you take me into the Red Queen's kitchen?"

"Not the best place to have a snack. If you're hungry, I know a place."

"No, Chesh. I'm not hungry. It's the only way I know how to regain my normal size. Hatter will be there soon, I hope. Won't you please escort me?"

"So, they *do* use the magic word in Otherland." He knelt to offer his hand for Alice to crawl aboard. "As you wish, Alice."

Her stomach tumbled at the thought of his magic compliance. "I've just heard of the blood oath. Have you been sworn to serve me as well?"

Cheshire's ear twitched. "I have no owners. No side."

"Sounds freeing, but lonely." Alice felt giddy from floating on an invisible hand, as if she were a bird outside of herself.

"It's the only way to live. I can doze unbothered in the sunlight as long as I like."

"Since you have no side, how can I be so sure that you're helping me and not the queen?"

"You can't." She heard him smile, but his face could not be seen. "Uncertainty can be as delicious as four and twenty blackbirds baked into a pie." He paused. "You're four and twenty now, aren't you, Alice?"

"Yes. I suppose I am."

"I bet you taste delicious," Oliver purred.

Her body didn't know whether to blush or run.

Alice slipped into the kitchens unseen, soon finding herself dropped from midair into a burlap sack of flour. She coughed at the rising white dust cloud as she stood. *Maybe the cat man was trying to eat her after all, innuendos aside.* She was ready to give Chesh a piece of her mind, but he was nowhere to be seen. She wasn't sure if she'd be yelling at empty air, so she stood and silently brushed herself off.

Alice gasped when she was suddenly scooped into a glass measuring cup. Her head poked out of the shifting flour once more, to see a pair of apprehensive red eyes aside softly curled, mid length, translucent hair and fuzzy white-pink rabbit ears. "Alice!" the man's nose characteristically twitched. "Is that you?"

"William?" she asked. "William White Rabbit, I remember you. I apologize, I must have been an annoying little brat at the time. I only caused trouble for you and your family."

"Not at all, Alice. We finally got to renovate my parent's house. We had insurance set aside for giant-based disasters, you know. Because of you, we got a brand-new kitchen out of the ordeal! But your demolition was entertaining, to say the least," he laughed softly.

"Thank you, Will. I'm certainly glad you don't hold a grudge. Why are you still working at the Red Queen's castle? Aren't your friends serving under the White Queen?"

"*Ssh!*" He turned around to check the empty kitchens for spies. "I've been working as the White Queen's agent for some time now. But there are ears everywhere. Luckily, mine are the biggest so I can hear them coming. I don't want you to blow my cover!"

"Brilliant!" Alice said in awe before recalling her purpose. "Will, have you seen Hatter today? He was supposed to meet me in the kitchens."

"Oh, dear, dear, dear," Will said worriedly. "Unfortunately, I hear that the guards have returned with a captive. It's possible that it could be him. The Red Knights are imbeciles. They only give the prisoners oyster shells, so you know he'll be hungry and thirsty. I can bring him a food tray later." He looked at the little lady in his measuring cup. "Why would you meet him in the kitchens?"

"Meeting him here would allow him to bake me some *Eat Me* cake and I could return to my normal size. I know it sounds preposterous. I don't see how that's going to work now. I wish we had time to think of a better plan..."

"Oh! I have a solution to at least one part of your conundrum." Will took out a crumb from his red velvet waistcoat pocket, next to his chained golden watch. "I have some *Eat Me* cake right here."

"Thank you, Will!" Alice reached, but the crumb was snatched away by William's white gloved hand when he heard the queen enter. She was frowning like a thunderstorm. *The Red Queen was learning to be quiet if she was able to sneak up on him like that.*

"Where is my tart, Sir White Rabbit?" The queen was beautiful, with hair as smooth and black as oil. But her dark eyes were like those of a wild beast. Alice recalled how quickly her pale skin could turn ruby; the fury and clamor with which she called for the heads of her enemies. The absence of the King of Hearts had her wondering if the monarch had stepped up to the chopping block as well.

"Your tart is coming, your Majesty," Will bowed. "I am currently in the process of making it."

"Why isn't the cook baking it?" The queen ran her fan under the rabbit man's nose.

"Unfortunately," William stuttered, "the cook finds himself without a head."

"It's so hard to find good help these days," the queen snapped her fan closed in frustration. "By the way," her eyes became alight with mischief, "the guards tell me they've apprehended that bothersome hatter."

72

"I'm glad to hear it." William kept his face stoic. "He was always mucking up your grand vision for Wonderland."

"Are you *truly* glad?" The queen raised a brow as she took a step forward. "I thought the two of you were friends."

"Once upon a time. But that time was long ago. He chose the wrong side if he can't appreciate a queen as full of heart as you."

Alice covered a snicker: *heartless was more like it.*

"Quite." The queen leaned over William's shoulder to look at the batter of her tart. "What was that?"

"What was what?" He hid the flour cup behind his back.

"There, in your hand."

"A measuring cup?"

"Inside of the measuring cup, *idiot.*"

William winced, "Flour?"

"Inside of the flour. Something laughed at me."

"Flour can't laugh, your Majesty."

"Hand it to me."

Will steadied a tremor in his hand as he anxiously handed over the cup.

"Hm," the queen eyed the contents before pressing them back into Will's hands. "See that you don't buy the *laughing* flour next time. It sours my appetite. Be quick with my tarts, Sir White Rabbit." She turned to leave. "Or... you can finish the sentence for me, can't you?"

"Yes, Majesty. *Heads will roll.*"

"You can be assured of that." The queen's train, black with red hearts, trailed behind her at her exit.

Will took a deep shaky breath. "Alice?" he whispered into the air after some time.

"I'm here," she said from his shoulder.

The rabbit man jumped. "How did you get up there?"

"I climbed up the back of your waistcoat."

"Excellent," Will breathed out. "You know, you've grown stronger than the last time I saw you. Smaller, but stronger." He smiled. "I'll take you to the dungeons to see the hatter once I finish baking the queen's tarts. Erm, may I put you in my watch pocket for safekeeping?"

"I've come to bring the inmate his supper." William showed the guard his tray with a tin cup and platter of bread and gruel. The guard wore black plate armor with the number four in the middle of a red heart on his breast. Alice couldn't see his face. But, from her place in Will's watch pocket, she could see the ring of keys hanging from the sword handle at his belt. As Number Four waved them into the cell corridor, William stepped closer to the guard so Alice could easily step onto the sword handle. Her hands wrapped around the dangling key ring. She carefully lifted it. It felt heavier than an anchor against the pull of gravity. *If she were her normal size, she could have lifted it with her pinky.*

"Pardon me, I've forgotten the water pitcher." Will brushed past the guard again, as was the plan. Alice clung tightly, with one hand on the chain of Will's pocket watch and the other on the key ring.

Alice faltered with the heavy keys. If she dropped them now, it would make an awful clang against the stone floor, altering the guard to her presence and William's double-crossing. All of their efforts would be for nothing and they would waste away in the Red Queen's jail cells. *Or worse.*

William carefully moved the food tray over to one hand and feigned checking his pocket watch. He placed Alice, along with the keys, back in his pocket.

"It's half-past the hour," said the guard.

"Thank you, Number Four," Will replied before dipping a pitcher of water into a nearby bucket. Alice let go of a breath she was holding when they passed the guard once more, hoping he was none the wiser.

Hatter's eyes were hard as he spied William, then curious. He blinked several times, as if he couldn't believe what he was seeing; as if he'd seen this hallucination before. "Alice," he gasped in a whisper. *"No fair!* I wanted to be the first one to put you in my pocket."

She laughed. "That's too bad. Next time. We're here to break you out, Hatter."

"I should thank you both. In fact- I will, once you use those keys to get me out of here."

"I shall leave it up to you, Alice," said William as he placed her down next to the tray of food. He then gave her the crumb of *Eat Me* cake from his pocket. "I don't want the guard to suspect anything, so I'll head out first." He stood and looked at his old friend. "Take care of her, Theophilus."

"That is something I can promise to," nodded Hatter.

Alice thought about how wonderful it would be to be back to her own size. Soon, lifting those keys would be as easy as turning a doorknob. She swiftly took a bite of the cake.

"Wait, Alice!" Hatter outstretched his hand.

A funny and flighty sensation filled her stomach as Alice felt the handkerchief dress tighten and unfold around her. Suddenly, she was far too large, and the fabric was far too small. She grew and grew until she had no clothes at all. Alice looked down and let out a soft noise of embarrassment as she covered herself with her hands. She hadn't thought this plan through, completely. She felt the blush spread across her bare body. At least Theo was the only one in the hall: inmates didn't serve long before the execution.

The view that Hatter received made him glad for the chains which held him back, and kept him steady to the ground. Her perfectly pert body was bare before him. Her narrow waist; the teardrop shape of her breasts. The soft pink of her nipples. He felt like the floor would give way. "I've never seen skin so beautiful," fell from his lips, before an ounce of sanity returned and he slapped a hand over his mouth.

"Thank you," she warmed, "but I'd rather it be clothed. Maybe I could share it with you another time?"

Theo's brows rose. "...You would want that?"

Alice outstretched one hand, her eyes begging him for her attire.

"Yes, of course," he closed his eyes as he rummaged through his hat and handed her the dress.

She slipped it up, over, and on, quick as a wink. "Have the guards hurt you anywhere? Are you feeling all right in there?"

"Considering the circumstances," he coughed, "I'm rather confused about how I should feel. But at least muchness seems to have returned to its usual size," he swallowed against his dry throat.

"You're the one to blame for this plan," she teased.

"I'm sorry, Alice." Hatter's hands held onto the bars. "I kissed you to keep you safe." He looked down in remorse. "Would you forgive me?"

"There's nothing to forgive." When Alice's soft hand came over his, Hatter felt a tremor of ease shudder through him.

His fingers cautiously found a way to be between hers. "What now?"

Alice sighed. "I don't think I could convince the court that I'd like to be a member."

"I wouldn't mind having you as my queen."

"Hatter," she laughed, "I don't know if what you've just said would be considered treason in this world. But I wouldn't mind having you to dutifully serve me."

Hatter could feel himself rising to the occasion. But now was not the time.

"Let's get you out of there."

"Our first priority should be the White Queen. Have you heard where they are keeping her?"

"William told me she's in the tallest tower."

The hatter nodded. "After you uncuff me, I can lead you there."

"No!" Alice shook her head. "You should exit through the sewers and rejoin your friends in the Whispering Woods. This is my job to do. I feel badly enough that you were forced to feel things for me through the White Queen's blood magic."

"Forced?" the hatter's brow crumpled. "Alice, I-"

"Guards!" The two heard the Red Queen shout as she turned the corner. "Seize her! I knew there was a little bug spying in my flour! *I just knew it!* Off with her head!" she screamed, "**OFF WITH HER HEAD!**"

Alice struggled to escape the guards' grasp. "Let go of me! *Let go!*"

"Your Majesty!" Hatter hollered desperately, "Your Majesty!"

The Queen of Hearts strolled by the cell with her arms crossed. "What is it now?" She had an exaggerated frown that brought wrinkles to her otherwise pristine face. "Are you mad that I've claimed another one of your so-called friends?"

"Quite the opposite," Theo swallowed. He had a plan, but it was risky; and not at all like the honest man he prided himself to be. He hoped that Alice would trust him enough to play along. "Why don't you let me measure the circumference of her neck? She has a delicate frame, not unlike your own. You'll want to get the blade sized just right for maximum impact. Wouldn't that be a glorious show- a new blade after all those dull beheadings? A rusty blade takes all the fun out of it, you know."

"Hatter!" Alice paled.

"Trying to get points for good behavior?" The queen gave a smile as she sauntered forward to squeeze the hatter's cheek. "You know, you might be of use. We're always in need of more good help in the Red Kingdom. I assume, since you introduced the plan, you have some measuring tape up your sleeve? Go on then," she released him, "be quick about it."

The numbered soldier and Knave released Alice from their grip and shoved her forward.

"Hatter?" Her eyes grew worried as she approached the cell door.

"Turn around, **spy**," he instructed, "so that your back is to the bars."

Alice fought the ice in her stomach as she turned to place her back against the cold bars. She had no reason not to trust him. *He loved her, didn't he?* She just had to believe in several impossibilities, and she was getting good at that.

Hatter's hands wrapped the measuring tape around her throat with gentle swiftness. Whilst gathering the size of her, Hatter pinned something expertly out of sight- inside of her collar. She felt his hands attach a cylindrical object before he withdrew. Her adrenaline spiked as he called out the number to the waiting crowd. The watchers clapped, as if her life were a game.

"Excellent!" The Red Queen smiled before gazing out of the barred window behind the hatter. "Oh, but the sun's going down and we haven't forged the correct blade," she petulantly pouted. Alice noted, with fear, that the shade of her lips was the same as freshly drawn blood.

"Majesty, might I offer further insight?" asked Hatter.

"You may."

"This woman has a fear of heights," said Hatter, slyly. "I would suggest holding her in your tallest tower or spire."

The queen sneered, for she knew the tallest tower already held one important prisoner. But the fact that this hatter would know that would be impossible. And the Red Queen did not believe in impossibilities. "Why would you tell me this information?"

"I quite like my hat, and I *would* need a head to wear it on. So, it makes sense that I would like to keep my head on my body for the foreseeable future."

The queen laughed. "You're more of a coward than the other Hatter's, aren't you?"

Alice's jaw dropped at the cruel audacity of the queen's words. She pulled against the guards in an effort to shut her blood-stained trap. Yet, they held her fast. All she could do was watch as Theo struggled to keep up his well-preformed act.

"Yes, Majesty," he said. "Bravery was what got them killed."

"I'm glad to see you can learn from others' mistakes." The queen paced. "Not to mention, you're quite the sadist, aren't you?"

"How so?"

"Wanting this prisoner to spend all night in terror before her impending doom?" The queen bit her lip as she placed her hands on the bars. "I'm beginning to like you, Hatter. There may be room for you at my side, yet." She reached in, to toy with a strand of his hair. "You can be my little pet. Would you like that?"

Alice could see the jealousy on the Knave's face at her suggestion.

"Most certainly," the hatter agreed.

Alice's stomach flipped as she gave the hatter one last pleading look. "Hatter!" she cried despondently as they dragged her away.

Hatter closed his eyes against the sensation, mentally imploring Alice to have faith. If she did not, he would have it for her: his Alice would succeed.

Chapter Six:
Of Dungeons and Desires

Alice continued to fight against the guards that held her fast. *What was that thing Hatter pinned to her back? What purpose did it serve in this twisted game?* She hoped that it was a fit of genius and not insanity that drove him to place himself in such a situation. After a long round of spiral stairs that made her stomach sick and head dizzy, she was tossed onto the floor. Her head spun as the door was barred behind her. Alice picked herself up to rush the door. She tested the knob and lock, which sputtered indignantly against her attempts. Banging the solid wooden door with her hands in one final fit, she turned to check her surroundings.

It was a bedroom with wooden tables, chairs, and a four-poster bed draped in flowery curtains. Back at home she would have considered her circumstances absurdly friendly compared to the castle's dungeons. Yet, here in Wonderland, what was mundane was often the most dangerous.

"Hello," a soft voice said, "Alice."

When she turned, Alice saw the White Queen. She was terribly untidy; everything on her person was crooked. She had the style of an older woman: a long lace dress with a shawl over her shoulders pinned by a brooch. Yet her face was that of a young woman in her thirties. It was as Hatter had said, the White Queen was aging in reverse. Her sandy hair had graying tips poking out of her updo. She seemed to be the opposite of the Red Queen. Alice liked her infinitely more. "Hello," she curtsied, "your Majesty."

"Arise, Fair Champion. Have you come to save me?"

"I have, but I'm afraid that I've created more problems than I've solved. Hatter and I have gotten stuck here, too."

"Are you certain that you are stuck? Is it possible that you have something that will get us out of this mess?"

Alice reached to the back of her neck, feeling what the hatter had pinned to her dress. It was a whistle: a reed whistle on a golden chain. What could she possibly do with a musical instrument at a time like this? It must serve a special purpose. She looked up to the White Queen for confirmation.

Her pale eyes shone like diamonds. "Galgalon."

"Galgalon?"

"The gryphon. My dearest friend."

Alice blinked. *Of course!* She recalled seeing one during her childhood adventures.

"Blow on the whistle with a pure heart and Galgalon will appear."

"How can I know if my heart is pure?" Alice looked down at the seemingly simple object. She'd had some thoughts that were decidedly impure lately.

The White Queen paused for a moment to think. Life could be understood in reverse, but for Alice it had to be lived forwards. "Have you ever wondered why the Red Queen is known as the Queen of Hearts?"

Alice thought. "I thought it was because she likened herself to the card in the deck."

"I suppose she always did have a thing for cards," the White Queen laughed, "but the true reason is that she has the power to manipulate hearts. That reed whistle was made with the queen's capabilities in mind- so that it won't fall into the hands of evil. Anyone who is able to withstand the Red Queen's manipulations will be able to call upon Galgalon."

"Is that so? How will I know if I've been manipulated?" Alice asked, suddenly fearful.

"Only one way to find out," the queen nodded at the whistle.

Alice brought the whistle to her lips and blew. She tried blowing harder, but she heard nothing in response. "I- it's not working. Could it be that my heart isn't pure enough?" Alice panicked. "Aren't you pure of heart, your Majesty? Maybe you could try?"

The White Queen laughed, "No, my child. I haven't been manipulated, but being queen requires a heart made murky from tough decisions. It has tainted my mind and soul. I gave that whistle to Theophilus because he had the most loyal heart I knew." She grasped Alice's hands. "He has given it to you because he thinks the same."

"I'm not so sure." Doubt doubled in her stomach.

"Through not knowing, you will know. Don't try to resist the fear. Don't try to prove yourself worthy, Alice. Accept uncertainty. Name it. Accept the discomfort. Welcome the feeling of it like a friend. Allow it. Nurture yourself. Then, close your eyes and try again."

Curiouser and curiouser... Alice thought as she felt the anxious feeling flutter through her. Anxiety was a rapid heartbeat, racing doubtful thoughts, and a sick guilty feeling in her stomach. This time, she invited the emotion to take a seat at the back of her mind before bringing the whistle to her lips once more.

"Alice," Theo sighed as he clung to the iron bars covering his rectangular window.

"Was that her name?" The Knave of Hearts leered. "Yes, you'll have a good view of her through those bars: right over the execution. You'll have a front row seat to watch her head cleave from her shoulders early in the 'morrow."

Hatter fought back a shiver.

The Knave stood back and sneered. "I'm onto your tricks, Hatter. I know you've got a thing for that pretty little lass. Who wouldn't? Why, I've gotten half stiff just thinking about her."

A vein jumped in Hatter's balled fist.

"When I have concrete proof, the Red Queen will have your head, too. Wouldn't it be romantic? A lovers' beheading, side by side? Unless we let the Bandersnatch or Jabberwock have a go at her first." The Knave chuckled as his prisoner cast him a dark glance. "Wouldn't that be a shame, Hatter? Those monsters from the Whispering Woods having a go at Alice before you or I ever could?"

"You will not speak of her!" Theo's eyes blazed as he strained against the chains which held him fast.

"Too easy," the guard's lip curled. "I think I will. I think I'll describe every little thing I enjoyed about the girl as I walked her to her tower prison. Her sweet-smelling curls, her cinched waist..."

Hatter gritted his teeth.

"The way her perky breasts bounced with each step. Her fiery eyes. Oh, I like a woman who fights back. I wouldn't think that you would as well. I didn't know you had the stomach to be such a turncoat. Yes... She trusted you, Hatter. We'll see what she thinks about that in the morning. That is, if her ticker is still ticking." The hatter slumped against the wall, resigned. There was nothing he could do. The Knave was done playing with his toy; unresponsive ones were no fun. He exited into the hall with a self-satisfied smirk.

Hatter kicked his abandoned food tray, causing it to clang against the bars. In the quiet darkness that ensued, he hung his head and slumped against his chains. His shattered breath came, "She trusted you... And it could very well lead to her demise." Theo wanted to drop it to the floor. He wanted to scream, and so he laughed. He laughed and laughed until his laughter resembled the pitch screaming. But his Alice had muchness. His Alice would be all right. She had to be. *She just had to.* "Alice," he wheezed as he wrapped his arms around his aching sides, "Alice!" he gasped, and a new onslaught came over him. He settled onto his bench to catch his breath. Hatter removed the constricting top hat from his head, still quaking with tears from sorrowful laughter.

"I knew I was mad, but I'm afraid I'm reaching levels beyond lunacy." He had to be, if he let the bloody Red Queen talk to him like that- as if he were her pet. He only wanted to be the pet of one person. Or, if she'd let him, she could be *his* pet. Only one person in this world could keep him grounded. He leaned his head back against the cold slab of a wall, gathering his thoughts. *Where was she now? Was she safe in the tower?* She must have been. He had heard the guards climbing up the spiral steps. When Hatter reached a conclusion about her safety, he sat up. Looking into the depths of his brim, he saw a welcome respite from his worries. "Alice..." he said to himself.

Her freshly worn pair of undergarments was still buried in his hat. Hatter took a deep hissing breath in, letting it out in a gust as he held them in his hands. *What was he doing?* He thought, guiltily. If Alice heard of this, she would... *like it*, he reasoned. She followed him to Wonderland. She wanted to share her body with him at a later time. How he wished she were here now, under better circumstances. He was drowning in miserable thoughts; he needed her like he needed air.

Theo, her voice echoed in his skull. *I need you **so** much, Theo.*

He breathed in the scent of her from the fabric. She was musk, and sweat, and **Alice**. Hatter ran an open palm over his growing desire.

She breathed, I want you now. I can't wait any longer.

Hatter released his straining member, stroking slowly from base to tip. "I would wait forever for you, Alice." His palm tightened into a fist as his strokes grew more frequent. He had seen her naked body and it was everything beyond his wildest dreams. He had previously tasted the salt on her skin, but he'd never been between her legs. *Dare he?* He ran his tongue along the lining of her panties, finding the lingering essence of her on his tongue. He tugged the fabric with his teeth, for he truly wanted to ravage her. He wanted to touch her like he had back beside his fireplace. The weight of her breasts in his hands; her areolas as soft as velvet; her nipples hard against his tongue. How would she sound when she reached her peak?

Yes! Just like that! Her voice resounded in his ears.

He wanted to hear her. He wanted to please her like she'd never known. He wanted to plunge into her slickness. He wanted to claim her as his own. He wanted to love and be loved. His heart quickened at the thought. Hatter wrapped the garment around his member, pretending to feel the weight of her body straddling him. She was hot, wet, and tight. She was everything good and right in the world, enveloping him. "*Ah!*" he jerked into his hand, spilling his seed and filling her up in his mind. That was all the reassurance he needed, even if it was imaginary. Hatter closed his eyes and leaned his head against the cool wall once more. He breathed until his quickened breath slowed and his heart returned to its natural rhythm. When he glanced down at Alice's ruined underwear, he smiled. She wouldn't be wearing those again. *His naughty Alice was currently walking around the castle with a bare bottom...*

"Oh!" The White Queen screamed as she covered her ears. "That was some explosion."

Alice looked around the quiet room in suspicion. "I beg your pardon?"

"You may want to hide behind the bed," the White Queen smiled as she quietly did so. Alice knew not to ask the citizens of Wonderland any questions and followed suit. Soon after, Galgalon burst through the tower wall. Stone and timber rubble tossed around the room as the mythical beast shook from its feathered eagle head and wings down to its furry lion feet and tail.

"Why didn't you scream at the time Galgalon burst in?" Alice asked as she retracted her hands from her head, dusting off a scratch.

"My child, I'd done all the screaming already." The queen shrugged and made no effort to shake the debris off.

"Alice!" Galgalon said as he pranced over. "I felt that it was *you* blowing on my whistle. I'm so excited to see you. Why, I haven't seen you since our visit with the Mock Turtle!"

"Likewise! I never knew your name was Galgalon," she pet the gryphon on the beak. "It's good to see you again, old friend."

"You're much taller than when you were here last time," the beast observed.

"I was just smaller until only a few moments ago," Alice laughed.

"Your Majesty!" The gryphon bowed when he noticed the White Queen in the room as well. "I've been on search duty, looking across the Red Queen's hiding places for you. I should have known that she cloaked the tower so I couldn't find you. Thanks to your whistle I could finally see it. Let's get you home. The Duchess has been worried sick."

The White Queen smiled as she climbed aboard the gryphon's back. "Yes, let us offer our presence to set her mind at ease."

Alice stood, staring at the door.

The White Queen continued, "In a few minutes, those guards will break down that door to find out what the cause of all that ruckus was. Shall we be on our way?"

Alice looked worriedly back at her friends. "What about Theo? Are we just going to leave him behind? Isn't it possible that they blame him for all of this?"

The queen closed her eyes to think. "You will need reinforcements. And a plan. You got lucky the first time. The Queen of Hearts will be ready for you now that she knows you're here, Alice. She will test your resolve; twist everything you know about yourself."

"All the more reason to save Hatter *now*." She stepped bravely, and foolishly, towards the door.

"Alice!" The White Queen opened her eyes. "If you step out that door now, you will find yourself without a head by morning. They're forging the blade Theophilus asked for as we speak. I'm certain he didn't actually intend for its use upon your nape- only you can make it so."

Alice's lips grew thin at the thought. Her hands itched to feel his once more; to know that he was safe by her side.

"The hatter has ingratiated himself to the Queen of Hearts. She is a naive and narcissistic queen: he knows this and exploits her faults well. Trust me. He will be all right until your return- I have foreseen it- but only if you leave this tower with us *right now.*"

Alice took a breath in and out, steadily, through her nose. Things seemed impossible. But the White Queen was the one who had taught her to consider six impossible things before breakfast; to consider anything but her tears. Hatter put his life on the line for the White Queen's Kingdom. If he could trust her word, so could Alice. "Very well. But I will **not** leave him here uninformed. I don't want him to think we've abandoned him. Then, the sooner we get you home, the sooner I can return to save him." Alice climbed aboard the back of the gryphon.

The queen gave a confident smile as she ordered, "Galgalon, take us to see the hatter!"

"Hatter!" Alice whispered, "Hatter!" The man slumped in chains on the bench before her was unresponsive. "Theo?" she spoke worriedly.

"Alice?" His voice came out cracked. "Alice! Alice, are you all right?" He noted the dried blood on her arm from the rubble. "Alice, are you bleeding? I killed you, Alice!" He wailed, "You're floating outside my window like a ghost. You should have known I was mad! You should never have trusted me, and now you've come back to haunt me!"

"*Shhh*, Theo... Oh, Theo," she cooed, "it's all right. I'm not dead. And I'm not floating, if that's what you think. I'm flying. We're riding on Galgalon."

"Galgalon! Your Majesty!" Hatter bowed in recognition as he looked further out his window. She nodded regally in response.

"I'll be back to free you. First, I've got to return her to her true seat at the throne. We can sort out the mess from there."

Hatter took a quavering breath, "Alice, my Alice. I'm so very proud of you."

"It's because of you, Hatter. After all, you lent me your whistle."

"I'm glad I could be of service." He gave a sad smile, "You know... Hatters have traditionally been pawns in the war between kingdoms. So, don't feel guilty, Alice."

"What do you mean?"

"I'm saying... It would be all right if this is where my story ends. If you can't return. At least I'll know that you and Wonderland will be safe."

Concern glistened in Alice's eyes as she reached for Theo's hand through the bars. "Don't say that, Hatter. There's still so much of your story that I want to know. Who would tell it to me if not you?"

"Oh, Alice, if only my story was yours to tell." Hatter closed his eyes, at peace, as his face felt the soft warm planes of her palm. "I bet it would be a pretty one indeed."

"It won't let it end here, Theo. Your story continues... I..." Was it really the time and place to say this? Then again, he was right. She may not have another chance. "I want it to continue on with me."

Just then, the armor of the Red Knights could be heard clanking underfoot. Troops were climbing the long spiral staircase. "She's escaped! The White Queen as well!" they shouted.

"What are you saying, Alice?" Hatter looked around in fear, "Go, *now*, or your story will end here as well! Your mission is far too precious to be held up by, talking to me." As a tear trailed down her cheek, he wished with all his might that his Alice would never cry again. When his hand came to wipe it away, she pressed a lingering kiss to his knuckles. He took in a breath and held it. For a moment it felt like a pledge of fealty.

"I'm saying, *I love you, Theo!*" She smiled feebly. "That means I'll come back for you. I always will. This is not goodbye, nor will it ever be." Her hand untangled from his own as the gryphon tore up and over the clouds. Hatter watched his Alice disappear into the night, his eyes never wavering from the point where she vanished. She would be safe now. All of Wonderland would be safe. His job was done. *So, why did it feel like his life was just beginning?*

"She **loves** me," he smiled out at the bars with a new type of laughter, "Alice *loves* me!" If he weren't shackled, why, he would dance into the night. He could scarcely believe it himself. *How had this angelic otherworldly creature come to care for a man so unhinged that his own kind would call him mad?* The thought caused him to pause in his jubilation. Now that Alice had admitted that she felt the same, could he control the madness within his own heart? Could he love her as gently and reverently as she deserved? He looked out at the full moonlight, shining behind the clouds. He closed his eyes. He didn't need to speculate. He didn't even know if he would survive the coming day. His Alice was safe and he had her love. "If that is all I have, then it's enough."

"Come now," a tail twitched against his ear, "that's not nearly entertaining enough."

"Oliver!" Theo blinked as he saw the grinning cat man. "I haven't seen you in ages and here you..." Hatter's eyes narrowed. "How long were you listening?"

"I heard it all." Oliver curled onto its back in midair. "I'm as surprised as you are. How you got one so fair as our Alice to fall for you, why, *it's astounding.*"

Hatter looked down and pursed his lips, unable to find a retort. What Oliver said was true.

Cheshire flipped back over, onto his belly. "Isn't she an odd one?" he hummed with his chin in his hands.

"Alice could never be odd," Hatter corrected. "She's all that's even."

The cat man grinned impossibly wider. "Funny, I wonder if she would say the exact same thing about you. Two people so close and yet so far." Oliver tilted his head. "A near catch, a near miss. You wouldn't bring about an unsatisfying end to my favorite game, now, would you?"

"Never." Hatter's smile mirrored that of his close friend.

"Duchess!" Alice hollered as she leapt from the gryphon in the first rays of light, "I have returned with the White Queen!" She nearly tripped over her feet as she ran to present the matriarch of the kingdom. The waiting crowd of citizens that had gathered to the familiar bird-like roar of Galgalon let loose a cheer. Alice kneeled as she waited to be received.

A look of teary gratitude overtook the Duchess' face, making her seem almost beautiful, as she broke apart from the crowd, running forward in excitement. The Duchess pulled the White Queen into a lasting hug that seemed to Alice more than friendship. She smiled at the love between them, though it tore at her that hers was still very much in danger. The Duchess then remembered her station, the White Queen laughing, as she curtsied to her monarch.

"You have served Wonderland well," the White Queen offered as she daintily pressed one finger under Alice's chin, tilting it upwards, "yet there is one more task I must ask you to fulfill."

Silas and Matias stepped to the front of the crowd. Silas' ears drooped at the hatter's absence. He then reached out to stop his hot-under-the-collar friend from pressing forward. "Where is he, Alice? Where is Theophilus?" His mouth faltered between anger and sadness. "We trusted you to protect him. You said you would keep him safe!"

"*And I will!*" Alice shed her own indignant tears. "He said that the White Queen's life was worth more than his own. I have returned her to you at the cost of my heart."

Silas and Matias paused to look at each other.

"Arise, Fair Champion, it is time to return our hatter to us," said the White Queen.

"Not alone, you won't," Matias stood beside Alice. "We're coming with you."

"I'll take all the reinforcements I can get," Alice nodded. "White Queen, have you foreseen anything? Are you certain that he'll return unharmed? The Red Queen has guards, a Knave, an army... Will the three of us be enough?"

The queen glanced at Alice's fretful eyes, "May I ask you something, Dear Champion?"

"Of course, My Queen."

"What is our Hatter to you?" The White Queen inclined her head slightly.

"He is…" Alice looked down and shook her head at the absurdity of it, "Everything."

The White Queen smiled sweetly, "True love is so rare in Wonderland."

"My Queen?" Alice blinked at the matriarch.

"My darling girl," The queen looked at her with soft eyes, "you wish to save your love?"

"More than anything."

"It takes the strongest of courage to fight for love. So many let a good love slip through their grasp when the going gets tough. If you have that value and determination, then fighting the Red Queen will be nothing at all."

Alice stood in contemplation for a moment.

"Who are you?" A soothing voice drifted towards her.

"Who am I?" She looked around, confused, "Why? Who are you?"

"I can't help you if you don't know who you are."

"Wait a minute," Alice spoke as she spied an older bearded man with butterfly wings in the crowd. "I know you… you were a caterpillar once. You blew smoke in my face and kept asking me who I was, like it was some sort of riddle!"

He smiled. "Well? Have you figured it out yet, silly girl?"

"I'm Alice. I've always *been* Alice."

"Exactly," the man said, knowingly. "Take all that love and confidence with you. It will be the best weapon in your arsenal against the Red Queen."

In the dark of the night, Alice set out beside Matias and Silas on the back of Galgalon over the Whispering Woods.

"I've had it with the Blood Queen," the hare man snarled. "I'm taking her out of the game, once and for all."

"Don't be so rash, Mati," warned Silas.

"No," Alice said. "Matias might be onto something. If the Red Queen were gone, then the war between kingdoms would essentially be over. Wouldn't it?"

"For once we agree," nodded the hare man.

"Silas, Matias; if I drop you on the roof of the throne room, do you think you could find your way in to capture the queen? We have the vorpal blade gifted to us by the White Queen, which can cut through her magic. Even if we don't kill her, we need to incapacitate her."

"It would be my pleasure," Matias sneered as he touched the hilt of the weapon at his back.

"I don't like violence," Silas swallowed. "But this war has gone on almost as long as I've been alive and I would like to see the end of it- outside of my dreams."

"Sometimes there are necessary evils," said Alice. "We're doing anything we can to make Wonderland a better place. We escaped earlier without Galgalon being seen, so they won't be expecting an attack from above. There will likely be guards at every entrance, leaving the interior throne room empty."

"The dome above the throne has four heart-shaped windows from which we can enter from," said Silas.

Alice and Matias looked at him.

"What, I can't be interested in the historical architecture of Wonderland?" Silas sighed. "You never ask me about my interests."

"Because you're always half asleep!" Matias clapped Silas' back. "But I'm glad you've got that interest, because it gives us a plan. We've got the rope."

"You two take care of the queen. Keep the vorpal blade with you to defend against her attacks." Alice dropped her companions off of Galgalon's back and onto the dome of the Red Castle. "I'm going to sneak in through the barred window to Hatter's cell."

"Good luck, Alice," Silas' hand parted from her own.

"Make good on your promise this time," said Matias as he began to set up the rope to rappel through the dome opening.

"I will," Alice ruffled the hair between his ears. If he was going to act like a grumpy little kid, then she would treat him like one. The march hare man was growing on her. She could see that he was only ever angry about the possibility of his friends being hurt. Alice couldn't fault him for that. She'd somehow come to find herself hoping to be considered his friend, too. Matias turned indignantly with a red face as he pushed his glasses up his nose. He watched Alice fly off with her tongue out. "You make good on your promise to subdue the queen, or you'll have to admit you're just as hopeless as I am!"

Silas covered a snicker.

"*Never!*" Matias called after her. Galgalon soared higher.

"Hatter!" Alice soon found herself at the outside wall of the prison ward.

"Alice?" The hatter looked startled by her presence.

"I've brought *Eat Me* cake and *Drink Me* potion," she lined them up on the sill between his bars. "I'm going to come in through the window and you can carry me to reach the keys.

I heard from William that the guards leave them on a post between shifts."

"Alice, I don't think..."

"We've arrived at the opportune moment when that should occur." Alice uncorked the potion. "I've come to rescue you and I won't take no for an answer. So- bottom's up," she said in cheers.

"**Alice!**" he stood as his chains clanked against the stone floor. As she began to shrink, she found herself cradled in the hatter's hands. He caught her before she fell through the bars. Her dress had landed further down, wrapping itself around his elbow. "Alice," he raised a brow as he looked her over, "you're naked."

"It's a necessary part of the plan to get you out of here. Besides," she flushed, "it's nothing you haven't seen before."

"*Oh?*" The hatter's brow joined the other at the top of his head. "Then, I would like to continue this rendezvous, but without the cuffs."

She knew he was mad, but her hatter was never forgetful. Alice paused for a moment. It didn't matter, she could consider his lack of memory when he was safe. "Won't you lend me out the bars so that I can reach the keys on the post to free you?"

"You mean these keys?" Hatter twirled them on a finger.

Alice's jaw dropped open and closed. "I- yes." Something was wrong. He had the key, yet he was still in chains. She tilted her head. As she looked at him, his smile was not his own. "...You aren't Theo, are you?"

His smile grew impossibly wider. "No, I'm not, little mouse."

"**Cheshire!**" she shoddily covered her body with her hands. "You could have said something earlier!"

"And *you* could have tried to say less," he harrumphed in a way which very much reminded her of Dinah flicking her tail. Her face grew hot. "Well, if you're here in chains, then where is Hatter?"

"I don't know. He went off. Something about a Knave."

Alice put the plan together. "He left you here in his place because he didn't want to arouse suspicion while he took out the head of the Red Knights..."

"Something like that." The cat man steepled Hatter's fingers under his chin with a smile. "Are you mad that he didn't wait for you?"

"A little," Alice miffed. "He would have been safer if he waited for me here."

"*You* would have been safer if you waited for him in the White Kingdom."

"I suppose you're right. But we each wouldn't have known if the other one was safe."

"What brave little *fools* you both are. The entertainment you've provided has been a meal, but I'm ready for dessert. Shall we hurry up and catch him before he hurts himself?"

"Hand me that *Eat Me* cake." Alice stuck out her hand.

Oliver turned Hatter's face towards the window, but he made no effort to move.

"Please," Alice smiled through gritted teeth.

"Of course," Cheshire acquiesced.

Alice popped the cake into her mouth, soon feeling herself growing again.

Once she had grown to her full size, Oliver observed Alice's naked form with a keen closed smile. "My. My. You *are* delicious, aren't you?"

The way that he said it with Hatter's face had her insides squirming. "I may be," Alice said, "but I'm not on your menu."

She didn't wait to ask for her dress as she yanked it from the crook of his arm.

Cheshire laughed softly through his nose. "That Hatter is one lucky cat to have a mouse like you."

"Thank you- I guess. I think we could serve him better if we fought at his side rather than waiting in a dungeon. What do you say? How do we get you out of here?"

Alice watched as the hatter walked forward. In one step, he blinked out of existence and the rusted chains on his wrists and ankles fell to the floor. The next step, Oliver was standing before her in Theo's top hat. His tail curled left and right. "Simple."

She tried not to gape. Cheshire may have been one of the most powerful in Wonderland. She was just starting to learn about its citizens, but she had to admit she was impressed. It was too bad that his allies and desires came on a whim. She had to keep him more interested in supporting her side than the Red Queen's. "Come on," she took the keys from his hand and jiggled them in the lock until she heard a click. The door swung open, and she held it for her companion. "I'm tired of playing. Let's end this game."

"What are you two doing here?" Number Four stood in the doorway.

Cheshire and Alice looked at each other with flat faces. She said, "Do you want to knock him out or should I?"

Cheshire stepped aside. "Be my guest."

Chapter Seven:
Of War and Love

The Red Queen wrapped her gloved fingers around William's black tie, pulling it loose. "You know what I want?"

"More tarts?" the rabbit man sassed as he held the silver platter aloft in one hand.

Her lips curled. "Nothing so sweet. I crave a little *spice*. Ever since the King of Hearts died, you know I've been lonely; I want a playmate. Can't I be your Mistress for the night?"

"Aren't you every night, your Majesty?" his brow rose.

"*Yes*." She smiled. "And it pleases me to no end. Get on your knees. I have a present for you."

"How can I reject such generosity?" William knelt on the red carpet, which was spread across the black and white checkered tiles leading up the steps to the throne. He looked up with half-lidded expectation.

The queen could see the pulse jumping in his throat. She withdrew a golden collar with a heart-shaped diamond on the clasp. William closed his eyes as he placed it around his neck. "I want to see you wearing nothing else," the queen commanded.

"Yes, your Majesty." He shed his necktie and unbuttoned his vest and pants.

"Yes, who?"

"Yes, Mistress." He stepped out of his clothes and left them abandoned on the floor.

"Mm, I like that." She smiled and motioned, "Come here, like a good little bunny."

William, wearing only his tail and collar, crawled on his hands and knees until he was at the queen's feet.

"My shoes have gotten dirty." She kicked out her black pumps. "Clean them for me."

William looked up hesitantly. As the queen reached down to touch his collar, a wave of pleasure rolled over him.

"Make them shine. You know how." Her gaze was half-animal. "Don't make me repeat myself. You know how the late king died."

"Yes, Mistress." The rabbit man held her heeled foot delicately. He ran his tongue across the patent leather as she leaned back on her throne.

"That's better." The Queen of Hearts smirked. "You're such a useful pet. Do it slowly." She noticed William stroking himself and sneered. "Did I give you permission to touch yourself?"

He panted lightly, "No, Mistress."

"What should I do about that?"

"You should," he breathed, "punish me."

"What a clever little bunny." She stood and beckoned. "Come here."

"How do we get past the Red Knights?" Alice whispered as she peered down the crowded hallway from around a corner.

"I have my ways." Oliver opened his hand to her. "Do you trust me?"

"No." She glanced down at his waiting palm. "Not really."

He smiled widely. "A good choice for a mouse to not trust a cat."

"For the last time," she put her hand in his own and smirked at his surprise. "I am *not* a mouse."

"Noted, but not obliged." The two of them blinked out of sight, soon reappearing in the throne room. What Alice saw scared her more than their disappearing act. Matias and Silas were tied up with the ropes they had used to rappel down on. William White Rabbit only wore a collar and erection as the Red Queen toyed with his ears. He sat atop her lap as she sat on her red and gold throne. The vorpal blade lay disregarded on the checkered tile floor. It hummed at her presence.

"Alice!" The queen stopped playing with Will's ears, much to his dismay. "So kind of you to join us! I thought your invitation got lost in the post when your friends showed up without you."

Alice quickly ran to pick up the sword, but was stopped short when she felt a weight on her head. She looked up to see that a golden crown had appeared.

"Well? What took you so long? You're the Golden Queen, aren't you?" asked the Red Queen.

"What do you mean?" Alice held the crown in her hands. Her mind was foggy. She couldn't remember ever wearing such an ornate piece of jewelry, nor could she recall governing a kingdom.

"That's right," said the Red Queen. "You're a queen, aren't you? That means you have to pass an examination to prove your worth to the citizens of Wonderland. All the queens are good hosts. Aren't we throwing a dinner-party tonight?"

"Dinner-party?" Alice closed her eyes to fight the buzzing in her head. When she opened them again, she wore a grand golden ball-gown that matched her crown down to the filigree. She stood in an ornate hall where there was no throne at all. "I didn't know we were having a party." Alice massaged her temples as she glanced nervously at the large ballroom. There were animals and people and people that were animals. There were even some flowers as well. She recognized none of them. *How was she going to be queen if she didn't know her people?*

"Shouldn't you say hello to the guests?" the Red Queen asked as she stepped aside to reveal Matias, William, and Silas dressed in their evening attire: knee-length coats with tails, each suit matching their hair color. "They're here to welcome you, after all." The men swarmed around her like bees to honey, each taking their turn to kiss her golden gloved hand. Matias and Silas grabbed at her waist and arms as Will began to breathe in the scent of her hair.

"Stop!" Alice cried as she swatted them off. "I'm not comfortable with this level of attention from you. *Please!*"

"You're not?" the Red Queen laughed. "I beg to differ. I've seen what's in your heart, Golden Queen. You wish to be loved. Isn't that nice? Your citizens have been pre-programed for you."

"I never asked for them to be! You're wrong, I never wanted to be hated *or* loved."

"Alice, Alice. You know- for a ruler- the answer is both, right? You're a hypocrite if you don't. Why, you're coming after *my* head for ruling over the hearts of my people when you have done exactly the same with a blood oath! Does the man you claim to love even truly love you?"

"He does!"

"In my kingdom, it wouldn't matter what he thought. He would love you just as much. Why take a chance with heartbreak, Alice? Wouldn't you prefer to have a fail-safe?"

"No." Alice shook her head. "I wouldn't. I'm not like you."

The queen tsked. "You're not so *high and mighty*, now, Alice. We're both on the same level, aren't we? Queens? Though your naivety comes from inexperience. Come," she placed her red gloved hand in the crook of Alice's arm and tugged her along sharply, "let me show you." The Red Queen paused to pick up her staff and stood before the three kneeling gentlemen. "Have you boys been introduced to my friend the scepter before?"

"No, Mistress," they chanted.

"No?" She looked on in mock surprise. "Ms. Scepter has always wanted to meet you. Look how eager she is..." The Red Queen let the smooth gold shaft trail up Silas' foot, ankle, calf, thigh, and stopped at the juncture between his legs where a problem was growing. "She likes you," the queen rolled the length of the scepter slowly back and forth against his crotch. "From the look on your face, I think you like her too. Should I be jealous?"

"No, Mistress. It's an extension of you, that's why it feels so good."

The queen stole a kiss that made Alice's heart revolt. "That's my good boy."

"Stop!" Alice called as she felt her insides squirming. "This isn't right!"

"Why?" The Red Queen smacked her scepter against her palm. At the top was a ruby heart encased in gold and diamonds. "Aren't they obeying me nicely? Don't they look like they're enjoying it?"

Alice could hear the wanton noises from the waiting crowd.

104

"I do, I want it," Matias exhaled.

"*Matias!*" Alice reddened in embarrassment for her tight-laced friend.

"And you'll get it." The Red Queen gazed at Alice for a moment before crushing the hare man's cheeks into a pout. "What if I leave a bruise on that *sweet* bunny ass of yours later? Would you take that for me?"

"Anything," he spoke.

"**Stop!**" Alice covered her ears. "Matias would never say that! Not to you."

"Oh?" asked the queen as her smile curled. "Would the blood oath make him say it to *you?* Tell her, Matias. Your queen commands you to."

"It feels so good," Matias writhed. "*Oh.* Alice, please, it's not enough... I need more of you. Just you. *Only you.*"

"Wait." Alice paused in contemplation.

"Yes?" the queen turned.

"I'm on the same level as you, aren't I?"

"You are," the queen smirked. "You can do just the same as I have."

"Then, may I have your scepter?"

"Of course, my dear." The queen paced over, her crimson dress trailing behind her. She handed over the staff, salivating to see Alice succumb to her baser desires.

Alice used the scepter to tip her friend's chin up, "You're a proud March Hare. Don't you ever debase yourself for anyone else." She then pointed it at the Queen of Hearts. "If I'm the queen, that means you aren't the only one allowed to give orders around here."

"*What impertinence!*" hissed the Red Queen.

"I order this fantasy to dissolve. Red Queen, you haven't truly seen into the heart of me if you can't get the details right. As someone very dear to me once pointed out, my color is not gold, *it's blue!*"

The colors of the ballroom swirled and faded around her as the throne room came into view. The scepter in her hand had transmuted into the vorpal blade. Matias and Silas were still in their bindings and William was still on the queen's lap as she sat on her throne.

"Welcome back, Alice," said Cheshire.

"You weren't in that fantasy," Alice said as she swung the blade to face him. "Why? What ties do you have to the Red Queen?"

"Maybe you just don't want me in your fantasies," the cat man pouted. "Dear Alice, I thought you liked me. How quickly the tides have turned. I must say, I'm disappointed."

"I am as well," said the Red Queen. "You had so much potential. We could have had fun ruling together. With me in charge, of course."

"How do you two know each other?" Alice asked. "Is he another one of your pets?"

"Rude of you to assume that *I* was *her* pet." The smile disappeared from Cheshire's face.

"...She was *your* pet," Alice came to the realization.

"Before the doddering Red King and temper tantrums, yes," he said, "she was. Though she was a bratty and bite-y little thing."

"I see," Alice said.

"We have differing opinions." The queen mockingly pet William's head. "He never wanted to be my little kitty."

"But you were all too happy to be *mine*," Cheshire showed teeth.

The doors to the throne room were suddenly thrown open, and all turned their heads to see a battle-worn Theophilus.

"Hatter!" Alice called as she ran over to him. "Are you all right?"

"I'm manageable," said the hatter as he clutched his side. "The Knave has been tied to her false majesty's railing by some measuring tape, awaiting later trial and dispatch." He perked up. "I can't wait to throw some books at him."

"You mean until the judge throws the book at him?" Alice asked.

"The judge can do that as well, yes."

"Welcome, Hatter," the queen grimaced. "Have you come to join in our fun, or to ruin it?"

"Stand back, Theo!" Alice held the vorpal blade in front of her in a fighting stance. "The Red Queen can cast magic to manipulate your heart."

The Queen of Hearts then let out an uproarious laugh, coming forth to knock the blade away with her scepter. "He hasn't told you, has he?"

Alice's heart dropped as she parried the attack. "He hasn't told me what?"

Hatter spoke from behind them, "Alice, I meant to tell you, I-"

"Hatters are immune to blood magic," the queen smiled as she held down the vorpal blade with all her strength. She had the knowledge to give her the upper hand. "That's why they've always been hired as messengers for the White King, because they won't be convinced. Hatters follow their own hearts, above all."

Alice let out her own mirthful laugh, thrusting her blade up as if a weight had been lifted off her chest. "Is that supposed to dissuade me? Am I supposed to fear, now, that the man who loves me can't be forced to love me forever? *Good!*" she spat out at the queen, pushing her back with attacks until she had been impaled. "Haven't you heard a word that I've said, Red Queen? *That wouldn't be love.* Even if he decided to leave me, I wouldn't want things to be any other way."

As Alice withdrew her sword, the queen let out a surprised cough. The succeeding coughs sounded something like mewls as she clawed at her throat.

"I hadn't meant to kill her;" Alice stepped back, "I only wanted to wound her. Is she all right?"

"You haven't cut through her body; you've cut through her magic, Alice," Hatter said. "That is a deep wound, indeed. Any façade that she's displayed will now fade away as she returns to her true form."

All Alice could do was watch as the queen grew smaller and hairier, soon standing on all fours in the puddle of her own gown. Cheshire stepped forth to pick her up in one hand.

"A kitten!" Alice said in awe. She was a rather cute one, too. Her fur was as black as her heart had been. Her eyes were as golden as her throne. "Are you going to be okay, Majesty?" Alice asked as she stuck out her finger, snatching it away before it was bitten.

"I've warned you that she was bite-y," said Cheshire. The kitten queen purred as it nuzzled its head along Oliver's chest.

"I think she likes you," said Hatter in disbelief.

"Who knows," replied Oliver as he rubbed the kitten behind the ears. "It's a very *convenient* habit of kittens: whatever you say to them, they can only purr in answer."

"I can see now why you disappeared into Dreamland for all those years," surmised Alice. "You were conflicted on where to lend a hand."

"Well," said Cheshire as he looked down at the kitten queen, "I know where I can lend one now. Until she annoys me, anyway."

"Come on," Alice grabbed her companion's hands. "Our work is done here. Let's go home."

"*Hey! False Alice!*" Matias yelled. "We're still tied up here!"

"Don't forget about us!" Silas cried.

William unabashedly walked up to the kitten queen. "Effective immediately, I tender my resignation. You're lucky that I couldn't cram all those tarts down your wicked throat like I'd planned. Now," he turned, "has anyone seen my clothes?"

A crowd gathered across the moat from the White Queen's castle to celebrate the defeat of the Red Queen. Streamers were hung from buildings and food carts had been set up on the cobbled streets. The heroes of the day stood on the lowered drawbridge of the castle, along with a single curtained item. Alice looked upon it curiously as the true queen stepped forwards to reveal what was underneath. It was the same ornate looking-glass that she had used to enter Wonderland. "My Fair Champion, this is your reward." The queen smiled gently. "The Duchess had lent this to Hatter on the condition that he find you. Now, the looking glass is your gift. This powerful portal will take you wherever you choose."

The crowd gave a noise of awe.

"Wherever?" Alice questioned as she stepped up to touch the glass. It rippled underneath her fingers, which she soon retracted. "You mean," she turned to the queen, "I can go home?"

Hatter took off his hat as he glanced up at Alice slowly. After all their adventures, he had thought... Well, he had hoped that she...

"Of course, my child." The queen's eyes traveled over the girl. "You may return to the other realm, unchanged, if that is your wish. You will remember Wonderland as a dream: the same as what happened when you returned to Otherland as a child."

Alice felt a roiling in her belly. *Otherland was where she wanted to be, wasn't it?* Her mother was there; her sister; her family. Sane persons. That was the world she had grown up in. That was the world she understood. It was the world where she lost her father. Though it wasn't the most wonderful place to be, it was, after all, her world: a dull world of sensibility and circumstance. She held the mirror frame tightly as she looked at herself reflected. Her eyes held her long list of worries.

Truthfully, what would become of her if she stayed? She had no idea what someone, or something, was meant to do. She had already accomplished her destiny to return the White Queen and secure the safety of Wonderland. The prophecy was completed, so Matias and Silas had been freed from their blood oath. Didn't that mean her presence was no longer required in this magnificent and dangerous realm? It was a frighteningly scary place that set her heart pounding. It was awesome and terrible. She hardly understood her feelings until she realized; it was just like falling in love. She turned towards Theo.

He looked down at the mirror briefly, then settled on her tea-and-honey eyes. For a moment he was a sponge, desperate to soak her presence in. She was going home: back to *her* home. A home in which doorknobs were silent and 'marveliferous' was not even a word. She would soon forget him. Even the sweetest dreams fade. She would not remember the love she held for him, nor the love which seeped from his very pores: the very thing which made him the Theophilus Hatter that he was today. He had followed his heart to her, like a true Hatter.

He would not tell her she could stay. *No.* They had both thought that there was no going back to Otherland. She would not throw away such a rare and unexpected opportunity. So, Hatter swallowed against the lump in his throat as he struggled to think of parting words- any words- that would be worth something at all.

"Fair fairing, Alice." *Was that his voice?* It sounded like a man in pain; one standing far away. He felt bad for that man. Hatter struggled to remain standing against the weight of her oncoming absence.

"Hatter, why are you wishing me off?"

"Well, you..." he began, but his words were interrupted by an impossible idea. "*You mean?*" His brows rose.

She smiled even wider, finally- the way that an Alice should smile. *For him.*

"That is to say?" He looked up, curiously, from under his lashes.

She laughed as she nodded. "Yes."

"Oh, Alice!" He scooped her up, spinning her into a kiss in front of the court.

The crowd hollered joyfully in response.

Her arms rested around his neck as her mouth met into his. "You know, you're making a contract with me by doing that."

"I'll make it a thousand times over," he grinned.

"You're my home, Theo. I wouldn't want to be anywhere else," Alice said. "If you haven't learned that by now, you're as mad as they say."

"*Even madder.*" He leaned in once more. "I can't even wait to show you how mad I-"

"**Ahem!**" The Duchess coughed into her hand. "It would appear they've skipped a few steps in the courtship tradition."

"It would appear so," smiled the queen.

"Hatter never was very traditional, was he?" laughed Silas.

Hatter looked back at Alice, sharing a smile, before returning her heavenly form to the ground.

"So, Alice," said the queen, "have you chosen where you belong?"

In another seemingly impossible moment, she grasped her beau's hand. "Here, in Wonderland, at Theo's side."

He returned her grip with all the love and gratitude he possessed.

"And do you approve of this match, Hatter?" The queen raised her brow knowingly.

"More than is physically possible," he smiled, "My Queen."

"Good." She smiled at him before turning to the girl in question. "Alice, if you walk through that mirror now, you will become one with Wonderland. You shall swear fealty to me. Then, you shall be free to pursue a match with our Hatter. Under these terms, you will only be able to return to the other realm unhindered for very brief intervals of time. Our bodies are not meant to withstand the banalities of Otherland. Does this sound agreeable to you?"

Alice responded without hesitation. "It does, your majesty."

"Then, you may pass." The queen waved her hand in gentle guidance as a calm settled over the rippling mirror.

Alice turned to Hatter, who gave her the most achingly understanding smile. Even now she knew she could back out, and he would love her no less. That very fact made her want him even more than she thought possible. She excitedly stepped into the looking-glass, feeling it splash like she'd walked face-first into a cool pool of water on a summer day.

The racing of her heart in her ears suddenly became the roar of the crowd as Alice opened her eyes. It felt as if she were doing so for the first time. The world had somehow shifted. She felt dizzy, like she'd just finished a dance that had gone all night long. She looked down to see the vividness of her blue dress. Her surprised gaze turned to her suitor who smiled at her profoundly.

"Welcome home, Alice," Hatter spoke admiringly as his finger traced her jaw. Alice shivered at his touch. It felt as if her skin receptors had multiplied.

"Champion Alice, you may kneel before me," the queen nodded.

Alice did as she was bid, taking a knee.

"Wonderland is forever grateful for your bravery. Will you continue to guide and protect its citizens?"

"I will."

The queen placed a magnolia blossom behind her right ear. "As these trees guard our kingdom, so may you. Please stand," she acquiesced. "Hatter," she smiled, "step forward."

Theo did so, holding his hat in hand.

"Is this your chosen mate?" The queen asked as she pulled Alice's right hand gently forward.

"Most definitely," Hatter smiled.

"And is this yours?" The queen spoke to Alice as she pulled Hatter's left hand forward.

Alice looked him over favorably, "Undoubtedly."

"Then," the queen placed her hand atop his, "let your love be fruitful. You may seal your union with a kiss."

The crowd cheered once more. There would be much merriment in Wonderland tonight, for the kingdom was safe and it had secured a valuable new subject. "Let us feast!" The queen ordered, to the response of renewed jubilations.

Silas crooked an arm around Matias, who looked back at the lovers and shook his head with a smile. William patted Oliver on the shoulder, who smiled widely. "Do you think there will be pie?"

As the others began their walk towards the castle, Alice leaned over and whispered to her chosen one's ear, "When she said fruitful, you don't think that she meant..."

"Why, it means our love will be bountiful. Don't worry, Alice, I will have enough for the both of us if you should find yourself in short supply."

"Hatter!" Alice spoke indignantly. "That's not what I meant." A redness crept up her ears.

The very sight of it sent the hatter's heart aflutter. He seemed to mull over the sentiment before giving her a startled glance. "*Naughty*, Alice." A sly grin hit his features.

"Forget it!" Alice said as she sped ahead. "Forget I mentioned a *single* thing!"

"Oh, Alice, you'll not get away from me that easily," he caught up to her in a single stride, placing an appeasing kiss on her head. She stopped and looked into his emerald eyes. "It means whatever you want it to mean, dearest. Anything or nothing at all."

"Will you allow me to show you what I want it to mean?"

Hatter looked at his bride with a new hunger. "By all means."

Alice smiled, took his hand, and led the way.

Alice exhaled from her spot atop the Hatter on his tweed sofa, "You kiss me like that any longer and I'm going to need to take you upstairs." She was surprised to find that his home was the same as it had been in Otherland. The White Queen and Duchess must have had very powerful magic to transport an entire house across worlds.

A thoroughly kissed Hatter gave a hungry stare in return. "Is that a threat or a promise?"

She grinned. "Both."

Hatter ferally picked her up. Alice squealed as she was hurriedly carried up the stairs. She didn't have time to look behind her as she fell onto a large down mattress, feathers flying around them, as Hatter crawled over her supine body. "Alice, I want to show you what you mean to me. I want to mark you as mine."

She whispered, "I'm already yours."

He grinned, hard cock twitching in response. "I don't think you understand." He backed her up against the headboard, hands opposite her head. Still, his body was not touching hers, always giving her an out. "I've wanted you my whole life."

Alice took a breath. "Do go on."

"I had to take myself in hand whenever I thought of you, and it was never enough. I worry that my love will be... overwhelming."

Her hands found his face as she imparted a kiss. "Never. Give me everything; give me all of it, all of you. I want it all."

Their lips crashed: kissing, licking, biting, and sucking. The contact elicited a soft moan from Hatter's chest. He kissed up her neck, breathing into your ear. "You'd like that?"

"More than anything…"

He kissed the flesh above her bodice. She gasped as he ripped it open to toy with her breasts, circling her nipple with his lips and tongue.

Alice's breath came quicker.

"Nothing to hide you, down here." Hatter's hand found her juncture. "I found your underwear inside of my hat. I came to my thoughts of you; I wanted you, astride me in the dungeon."

"It would seem I rescued you from there more than once," Alice teased.

"I got jealous thinking of any guard who could see the sweetness under your skirt." Two fingers traced over her opening: his expression full of awe and curiosity. "You're so wet for me…"

She bit her lip. "I've been wanting this for a long time."

"How long?" His thumb circled her clit as his other hand toyed with her chest.

"I- I don't know."

His Alice was embarrassed and it made him *hungry*. "How long have you wanted to ride my cock, Alice?"

"Since Otherland," Alice moaned. His hands felt so good.

"Is that so?" He gave a satisfied smile. "Have you ever touched yourself to me?"

"Please, don't stop…"

"I'll keep going when you answer."

"I… *Yes!* Yes. Plenty of times. I dreamt about you doing me up against a tree in the Whispering Woods."

"That's my Alice. My naughty *good* little Alice." He kissed the inside of her thighs, tongue trailing along her leg, but never getting close enough. "Tell me, was my mouth hot on you in your dreams?"

She nodded, frantically.

116

"Are you mine?"

"All yours. Always."

He swept up her slit in broad warm strokes of his tongue. Hatter circled her clit with the tip of his tongue, sending electric up her spine as his plush lips applied sucking pressure. Alice's head rolled back as she made her pleasure known. Hatter's tongue slipped between her folds, his nose nudging her clit as he made wanting noises. "You taste so good, Alice," he moaned as he trailed her sex with his tongue.

Alice grasped the board behind her head as he went down on her. She was finding it harder to breathe- her legs shook as his honed fingers entered, beckoning her pleasure center. She cried out when he sucked an even pressure on her clit, leading the world to fall into splotches of color as she came apart on his face. As the aftershocks sputtered through her system, his mouth was still kissing up her sex. Hatter wiped his mouth on the back of his hand before he leaned over to kiss her forehead.

"You're really good at that," Alice breathed.

"It pleases me to please you to no end, Alice," he grinned.

"I want to please you, too," she trailed her hand over the bulge in his trousers. It felt exactly as it had in her dream. She wondered how thick it would feel in her hand.

"You don't have to-" Hatter looked impossibly shy. "Your pleasure is enough to satisfy me."

"Is that right? Well, I won't be satisfied until I see you come undone, completely."

His mind was already unraveled. "Anything for you." He unbuttoned his waist, pulling out his hard length which reached to his belly button.

Alice greedily wanted more. "Touch yourself for me."

He passed a hand over once, then twice, as his other hand gripped the headboard behind her. He whined as his eyes were smoldering on her and his hips slowly pumped forward.

"It looks like you want to say something," Alice teased. "Ask me and I just might do it."

"Touch me, Alice. *Please*," he moaned.

"I'll do more than that," she smiled, lowering her lips to kiss his shaft. "Can I put you in my mouth?"

He leaned backwards, dazed, as if the phrase were impossible. Then, he nodded with a blush. His hot and heavy cock was the most beautiful thing Alice had ever seen. The pink tip contrasted with the pale base of him. He was already dripping with precum from the foreplay of getting her off. Her breath on him was enough to make him shiver. Hatter was sensitive. She would go slow. Alice ran her finger up the underside of his shaft, causing him to shake. His head was like velvet. Alice kissed him again, lightly, watching his wanting expression as she stuck out her tongue to taste him.

Hatter let out a soft noise as his hips pressed into the contact. She smiled before she took him into her mouth. He groaned, "Alice," and placed both hands on the board behind her. She sucked slowly up and down his shaft, cupping and cradling his balls in her hand as she did so. "I don't think I can last in your mouth;" he leaned over her, "take me inside of you; I want to feel you, please."

Alice released him, wiping her mouth before imparting a kiss. She pressed him down, backward on the bed, before straddling his waiting cock. "Are you sure you want me?"

"More than air..."

She positioned him at her entrance, lowering herself slowly. His eyes were watching hers, his mouth briefly groaning, as she took him into her body. She felt her pulse around his girth as he throbbed within her.

118

"Alice," he sat up to kiss her neck as her legs wrapped around him and she rocked on top of him, "Feels so good... So good." She could feel a tear from his eye on her shoulder. Alice cupped his face in her hands and kissed his closed eyelids, tasting salt. He tilted his face until his lips met hers; his tongue traveling over her own. She sighed pleasurably when his rough thumbs traveled over her nipples.

Hatter brought his lips to her chest, sucking as his hips bucked beneath her. Her body met his, bringing pressure down onto her clit with their meeting bodies in every thrust. Hatter looked up to see Alice looking down at him; her heart was open and more vulnerable than he'd ever seen in their time together. The sight took his breath away. "I love you, Alice Everly," he breathed. "You're mine. All mine. Always. I promise to work hard to never let the thought cross your mind that you should be anywhere else."

"Good." Alice tossed her head back in bliss. "Don't stop. Don't let me go."

"Who do you love?" He ground into her, sparking signs of another orgasm. Alice moaned as he tweaked her nipple. His jealousy was maddening. "Who do you belong to?" His breath came in hot bursts against your skin. "I can feel you want to cum. Feel you pulling me in; milking me. But you'd better cum," he thrust, "with my name on those perfect lips."

"Ah! Theophilus!" She groaned, "Hatter!" Her body shook in wave after wave of pleasure.

His full name pulled from her cumming lips sent a thrill straight to the base of him. "That's it, that's my Alice. *Ah.* I'm going to cum if you ride me like that." His voice wavered as his head found her chest, his arms pulling her in. "I'm going to cum for you. *Oh.* Can I cum for you, Alice?"

"Yes!" Alice moaned, "*Cum for me*; inside of me!"

He swiftly laid her on her back, his hips snapping to meet hers as the sounds of their pleasure mingled. Watching the abandon on the hatter's face and hearing his rumbling moan made her wet all over again. He pumped until his body grew rigid, spilling himself inside of her as he made noises of satisfaction against the pillow near her ear.

They caught their breath. Hatter gave a smile and kiss before lying down beside Alice. Their bodies buzzed in the warm afterglow. Alice closed her eyes as she curled against her groom. A giggle stalled in her throat as she thought of something apropos to say. "That was marveliferous."

At her use of the Wonderlandian word, Hatter held her impossibly closer and peppered kisses on her head. He didn't know what he did to deserve such unfettered devotion, but he was sure glad that he did it. And he would return Alice's efforts in double, every day until his ticker stopped ticking. "*Marveliferous*," he repeated with an easy smile on his face. "That describes my life with you."

Made in the USA
Coppell, TX
14 May 2023

16827653R00080